The Red House

Also by Christopher Bowden

The Blue Book
The Yellow Room

The Red House

Christopher Bowden

LANGTON & WOOD

Distributed by Gardners Books, 1 Whittle Drive, Eastbourne,
East Sussex, BN23 6QH
Tel: +44(0)1323 521555 | Fax: +44(0)1323 521666

British Library Cataloguing in Publication Data
A catalogue record for this book is available from the
British Library.

ISBN 978-0-9555067-2-7

Typeset by Amolibros, Milverton, Somerset
www.amolibros.co.uk
This book production has been managed by Amolibros
Printed and bound by T J International Ltd, Padstow, Cornwall, UK

Players should be immortal, if their own wishes or ours could make them so; but they are not. They not only die like other people, but like other people they cease to be young, and are no longer themselves, even while living.

William Hazlitt 1816

Prologue

---

*H*e woke breathless, sweating, wrenched from sleep by the terror of impending confinement. It was that room, always that room. What if he had been kept there longer or forced into a smaller place, a dank, dark cell that excluded the light of day, left to starve or rot? Had he not been told he would not be missed?

Colin Mallory looked at the foetal form beside him, the gentle rise and fall, sleeping undisturbed. Perhaps he had not cried out at all. He picked his way to the window and parted the velvet curtains. The blue-grey street below was still, shops shuttered, cafés and restaurants closed. A lone cyclist penetrated the gloom, coursed through winking traffic lights without a glance, and was gone.

It had been a while now. He thought he had got over it, left it all behind, when he started afresh. It was all so random. There was no pattern that he could discern, no obvious trigger. Just an underlying sense of unease. Weeks would go by, weeks of relative peace, and then it happened again.

A distant siren. A cat moving in and out of shadows. He looked at his watch and let the curtain fall. It was no good; he was not going to sleep again now. He pulled on clothes in the bathroom light, hoping the whirr of the fan would not disturb, inched open the heavy panelled door and let himself out. The clowns followed his progress, staring unsmiling from frames placed at intervals along the corridor, sinister and subdued at this hour. He took the stairs that spiralled to the lobby, nodded at the man who woke with a start at the desk, and stepped into the chill of the Rue des Bouffons.

The familiar streets looked different now, drained of colour and movement and life, overwhelmed by the bulk of apartment blocks, pallid and austere. He passed Le Navet d'Or, the café where they had had breakfast that first day and every other since; shuffled through leaves gathered at the gated entrance to a small park; crossed the silent boulevard, squeezed by cars mottled and streaked with moisture; and headed east towards the lightening sky.

It had been a gamble, coming here. An act as impulsive as the others that had changed the course of the last few months, for him, for both of them. So far, so good, but where it was leading it was hard to say. At least people knew where he was, this time.

He found himself where the market had been, not far from the place the canal flowed from view and continued underground towards the Seine. He had kept to the margins, avoiding crowd and crush, content to watch, thinking of that other market, the one in Oxbourne, and the damp March day he had seen her picture through a window.

One

---

*H*e knew it was unwise to come this way, confined, constrained, pushing past bodies and baskets until he was through. But it was the most direct route, the quickest way to reach the café on the other side.

He slipped between shoppers seduced by home-made fudge and chocolate brownies on the left, stuffed olives and pickled walnuts on the right. He dodged the display of goat's cheese, skirted boxes and bags of organic vegetables, and slid over wet cobbles by the flower stall. Tulips of purple velvet jostled those of ivory and a curious green sheltering in plastic buckets beneath ranks of clematis and unnamed shrubs just coming into bud.

He steadied himself against a lamp post at the pavement's edge, dizzy and short of breath. Stray curls of dark-brown hair stuck to his forehead. He was still not good at crowds, felt trapped, had to get out. He pressed against the lamp post, its fluted form reassuringly solid, calming, as he looked back across the square.

Awnings striped and plain billowed gently in the hint of a breeze; lightweight clothes, trailing from hangers, spun slowly to and fro. The whole market seemed afloat beneath a thinning sky.

He too felt light-headed, disembodied, outside himself. He had to sit down. The café was only a few steps away, held tight in an orderly row facing the square, between the Millefeuille pâtisserie and a vacant shop previously offering scented soaps and candles of exceptional pungency. It was an offer that the residents of Oxbourne had found eminently resistible.

The café was much as he remembered it, tiled walls decorated with small vignettes, some violet, some blue, depicting fine specimens of the sort of animals whose carcases used to swing from hooks at the back in the days when this was a butcher's shop. Fixed to a column near the till, a wire rack stacked with newspapers, neatly folded, titles outermost, running the gamut from *The Oxbourne Advertiser* to *The Wall Street Journal*. Designed to be seen rather than read, he reflected, as he installed himself at a pitch pine table reassuringly close to the door. He leaned on an Aberdeen Angus, a chunky beast staring moodily at the Tamworth that stood its ground three squares to the right, and looked about him.

In the far corner, a bearded man staring at the laptop, the light of the screen caught in his glasses, giving them a disconcertingly opaque appearance, almost as if he had no eyes at all. The thought was unsettling. Colin turned to an intervening table. A family laden with market purchases, bags tilting and bulging around them, parents sharing the contents of an oversize cafetière, children sporting thin brown moustaches from the mugs of hot chocolate which they held with two hands.

He extracted a slim volume of Steinbeck short stories from the inside pocket of his bottle-green velvet jacket, bought in a Boston thrift store in which clothes were arranged not by size or type but by colour, reflecting the sequence of the rainbow. He laid the book on the table and picked up the menu.

A hatchet-faced waitress with lifeless near-blond hair brought him coffee and a blueberry muffin in double-quick time.

"Enjoy," she said, in an accent reminiscent more of lands to the east of the Danube than of those to the south of the Thames. It was an instruction, not an expression of expectation or hope or desire.

He gazed at the surface of the coffee for a while, its iridescent film like an oil-stained puddle, a peacock's tail. He dripped milk from a small white jug, stirred half-heartedly, and looked out of the window. His neck and shoulders ached. It couldn't have been overwork. He did no work, though he was thinking about it. He needed to relax, unwind. It wasn't easy coming back, expected to slot in and carry on as if he had never been away, reverting to his teenage persona well into his twenties.

He saw a raddled man in red baseball cap perched on a folding stool outside the empty shop next door. Ash-grey hair was drawn tightly in a pony tail and threaded through the back of the cap. The man's eyes flicked between a large sketch pad, held on his knees at an angle of some forty-five degrees, and the small girl sitting opposite. She was trying not to giggle. Colin watched as pencil skimmed across paper, bringing her features rapidly to life. The man finished with a flourish, presented the drawing to the child's delighted mother, and pocketed a ten-pound note.

As a small crowd of on-lookers dispersed, the man removed other pictures from his battered portfolio, smoothed their cellophane wrappers, and fixed them to a board with clips and pins. Colin gulped lukewarm coffee and was preparing to tackle the muffin when he glanced again at the board, now propped against the lamp post that had supported him not long before. He did not linger on the corgis, the still life or the smiling postman but the drawing of a girl struck a chord. More than a chord. He had to have a closer look.

"I'm coming back," he called to Hatchet Face as cup crashed to saucer, spattering the cover of his book, and he scrambled up and out.

Her face was thinner than it used to be, tauter somehow, almost gaunt, and the eyes seemed troubled. The hair, once long and flowing, was cut roughly short. Almost hacked, he thought. Yet it was surely her, staring anxiously from the picture pinned to the board in front of him. Bryony. Bryony Hughes. They had gone their separate ways six years earlier with promises to keep in touch. He had not seen her or heard from her since.

"When did you do this one?" he asked the man. "I think I've seen her before."

"Last time I was here, mate. The Saturday market."

"Why did she leave the drawing?"

"She ran off before I'd finished. Strange girl. She appeared from nowhere and sat down without a word. Wouldn't stay still. Kept looking round."

"I wonder why she wanted her portrait done."

"I don't think she did. Seemed like she was passing through, taking refuge for a while. She hardly seemed to know I was sketching her."

"Why were you?"

"There was something about her. Not your typical Oxbourne Saturday shopper. And business was a bit slow, to tell the truth."

"She doesn't look well."

"She looked worse in the flesh, I can tell you. A lot worse. She was pale. Deathly pale. And dressed entirely in black. Clothes were all crumpled, as if she'd slept in them. Did you say you knew her?"

"Years ago. We were at the same school. St George's, on the other side of the bypass. She had long golden hair then. Always brushing it. One of the masters called her The Rhine Maiden. The name stuck, though he didn't. He was knocked down running for a bus after the house music competition."

"Ah, the Lorelei. Beautiful but deadly."

"How much do you want for the drawing?"

*

Colin put the pans to soak and sat back at the kitchen table. A large clock, removed some years ago from the waiting room of Oxbourne station, ticked softly on the opposite wall. He knew that if he went into the sitting room he would fall asleep. He had only meant to have one glass of wine with his spaghetti bolognese, sauce conjured from the jar washed and inverted on the draining board, but somehow half the bottle had gone. He looked again at the sketch propped against the pile of newspapers destined for the recycling sack. The man had been keen for him to have it and would take no money.

The Bryony he remembered was happy and confident and extrovert. The leading actors in the school, they were inseparable at one time, spent their days together and many of the evenings too. Colin and Bryony – Col and Bry – an item, people said, one and indivisible. But it was not to be. Acting had brought them together but it also drove them apart. For him, it had just been a hobby – and a way of avoiding games. For her, an all-consuming passion. She was restless and ambitious. Getting on meant getting out, she had explained tearfully in the woods that afternoon; she could not let other people hold her back. Not even him.

She had gone to drama school straight from St George's and everyone predicted a bright future. Since then, nothing, though his mother once claimed to have spotted her as a nurse in the pilot episode of *Hospital Corners*, a sitcom in which two young mothers were mistakenly given each other's babies – with hilarious consequences! They never made the series.

Perhaps, he thought, he had accepted rejection too meekly at the time, been too passive. He should have made more of an effort to hang on to what they had. Would it have made any difference? Unlikely. She had made it clear he was part of a past she was leaving behind, that there was no future for them together. Yet he still felt guilty that he had made no attempt to trace her over the years, to find out where she was or what she was doing. He had been away himself, of course, but even so. When he considered how things had once been.

The house in Milton Lane had been sold after her parents died. That much he had heard from his sister, Clare. Why had Bryony come back? Was she still in the town? Improbable. It was nearly a week since the man with the sketch pad had seen her. And where had she stayed? With someone she had known at St George's? Or had she slept rough, remembering what the man said about her clothes?

Whatever the answers, it looked as though she was in trouble and needed help.

Two

What colour is it today, Mrs Nolan?" asked Colin, easing himself on to a chair lodged between table and wall in the Mallorys' kitchen. He had slept badly and had a headache. He removed a large banana from the fruit basket and placed it in front of him, adjusting its position with a forefinger so that it was roughly parallel to the grain of the wood. He shifted in his chair and took a newspaper from the top of the pile whose transfer to the recycling sack was now imminent. He glanced idly at job advertisements well past their application dates: strategy development assistant; customer insight analyst; website marketing executive... . Nothing that appealed to him at all.

"It's Friday. I'm here on a Friday."

"That'll be brown, then. Not dark brown like coffee or chocolate. It's more orangey than that. Like a ten-pound note." He thought of the one changing hands outside the café the day before. "A warm, reassuring colour, don't you think? Unlike Thursdays. They're blue-grey and depressing."

"I'm sure I don't know what you're talking about," she said, delving into the cupboard under the sink to retrieve a bottle of bleach. Her hair, this morning, was an unusual purple-red, reminiscent of plum or damson. "Is this something to do with that philosophy you've been studying?"

"No, no. Words have colours. Surely everyone knows that. So do letters and numbers."

"Not in my family, thank you very much."

"We used to argue for hours. My father said Friday was magenta. Clare insisted it was green. We all saw them differently."

"I never have this from your mother."

"She can taste words too. She used to say Colin tasted like fish. I'd rather have been called something else."

"You're having me on."

"How about Maxwell? Max Mallory. Has a certain alliterative charm, I suppose. Liquorice, would you say? Or maybe vanilla."

"Would you be any nearer to getting a job?"

"I'm thinking about it."

"You can do too much thinking. You need to get out of the house more. What about teaching?"

"The position of Court Philosopher would suit me. 'Philosopher Royal': sounds good, doesn't it? I could offer deep thoughts and considered opinions on matters great and small with a double-helping of wise counsel on state occasions."

"Court Jester would be more up your street," said Mrs Nolan, putting the bottle in a bucket with her rubber gloves and heading for the stairs. Cleaning for the Mallorys for a dozen or so years had given Geraldine Nolan licence to express her views a little more bluntly than might have been expected. Nobody minded. Anyway, she had problems enough of her own, what with husband Bill doing another stretch and her grown-up sons occupying the narrow ground between feckless and totally useless.

Colin knew she was had a point, though. He did need to get out of the house and do something. Not just amble about town avoiding crowds, drinking coffee and reading in quiet corners. But what? Nothing seemed right – and doing nothing was a lot better than settling for second-best.

He was not lazy by nature. His academic record – scholarships, prizes, Harvard – spoke for itself. Neither did he lack ambition. Not in principle. But ambition, he told himself, could not live in a vacuum. To be manifested, it had to be applied. At school and university he had had something clear, time-limited on which to focus and he had delivered the goods. Now that structured existence had come to an end, he felt at sea. It was just a question of finding the right thing, or spotting it if it hove into view. If only he knew what it was. Anyway, he lived in the house rent-free and had his grandmother's inheritance to fall back on, if all else failed. So what was the rush?

He re-read the postcard from his parents delivered that morning. They had made it to South Dakota, were staying in the Black Hills, and had seen a bald eagle at Mount Rushmore. It was not so long ago he had been there himself, travelling the Mid-West with that Chelsea Peterman, a law student he had met on the plane to Minneapolis. They had parted without acrimony in Jackson, Wyoming, after an eventful forty-eight hours in Yellowstone National Park involving a geyser, a puncture and an ill-tempered coyote. He placed the picture of four large Presidential heads on the pine dresser, retrieved his banana, and went to find his jacket.

The sun was shining as he left the house at a time when he was normally still in bed. He threw the banana skin in the wheelie bin lurking behind the privet hedge, paused to admire the violets and primroses that had taken over the lawn, and set off slowly up the hill. Number twenty-six was a large house, semi-detached but double-fronted, completed some months after the relief of Mafeking, in honour of which the road had been named. Most of the similar houses in Mafeking Avenue had since been converted into flats but the Mallorys had held out against the rising tide of estate agents' cards assuring them that they had long lists of clients urgently seeking tastefully appointed properties such as their own. In the vicinity of number sixty-four, bristling with coach lamps and blowsy camellias, he was greeted breathily by long-time resident Mavis Campion moving towards him with impressive speed on her shiny new adult tricycle. Her Siamese cat Victor surveyed the scene from the wicker basket at the front.

"Good to see you back, Colin. It's been too long. I shall bring rock cakes when next I bake a batch."

His spluttered response went unheard as Miss Campion receded fast in the direction of Oxbourne town centre.

The entrance to the woods lay at the end of a quiet road, little more than a gap between blue-green holly and twisted oak. Negotiating an awkward gate designed to deter visitors on wheels, he stumbled forward and steadied himself on a concrete post. Fallen berries, like spots of blood, stained the damp earth through clouds of breath. The air was still cold this crisp March morning.

The woods were managed, but not over-managed, and lacked the nature trails, helpful signs and picnic tables that defaced other sylvan settings in the borough. He struggled to remember the way to go. He chose the path to the right, discreetly marked with quartered logs, dark and dank and greened by moss. Here and there, remains of houses long since demolished were visible beneath ivy and bramble. Clumps of tall bamboo, vestiges of gardens of the past, stood like silent sentries, incongruous beneath the canopies of beech. Wide banks of rhododendrons, neat and budding, reinforced the sense of intrusive domesticity.

A dark glint beyond the path. He had found the pond, pinched by silver birch, trunks shimmering oyster-white in the clear, sharp light. A trace of moon, pale and pockmarked, high above a solitary pine. He lowered himself onto a bench set on a small stone plinth well back from the black surface of the water. According to the inscription on its back, the bench had been donated a couple of years before in memory of one Marjorie Ashmole, 'who knew this place'. He knew this place too. He used to come with Bryony. They shared the old seat that was here, silver with age and rough with lichen, before it finally rotted and fell apart. They would learn lines together, read their books, throw lumps of bread to the gently quacking ducks or sit silently watching the sun slide behind the trees, the light as soft as the copper-pink of the bracken in the woods.

He sighed at the remembrance of things past. And past they surely were, of their time and of their place, to be evoked, recalled but not repeated or renewed. Yet he wanted to know, now that he was back, to find out what she had done, what she was doing, where she was. It mattered, even after six years apart, with not a word between them.

The path continued through a region of hazel and sweet chestnut, desiccated shells like ginger sea urchins on a bed of curling leaves. He was heading for Milton Lane and the house where Bryony used to live. As he neared the end, the path dropped suddenly, exposing tree roots high on either side. They looked innocuous enough in the light of day but at dusk their twisted and contorted forms harboured elves and goblins, sly and leering, snatching and scratching, winning the unwary with gifts of gold and poisoned fruits. Or so he and Bryony used to pretend as they skittered past, arm in arm, their imagination fed by an exhibition of books illustrated by Arthur Rackham held one term in the school library.

His pulse quickened as he neared the house. But what he saw was not what he remembered. Milton Lodge, the name barely legible on the powdering pillars that flanked the entrance to the drive, was a gloomy place, untidy and overgrown, surrounded by laurel and yew and other trees that did not lose their leaves. The gothic detail that had made the house seem lively and eccentric now looked sinister and uninviting. The paint was peeling and the gutters sagged. A tyreless car balanced precariously on piles of bricks in a patch of oil-stained grass.

As he turned to go, shaken by the state of the place, a first-floor window shrieked open. A large head pushed through the greying nets.

"Can I help you, young man?"

"I just…I wondered if you'd seen a friend of mine. In the last few days."

"Any particular friend?"

"A girl, with long…I mean, short…blond hair. Roughly cut."

"I think you'd better come inside."

A scattering of red rubber bands, discarded by successive postmen, marked a trail across the tussocky grass. Colin followed it to the porch, a fragile structure whose pitched-roof form loosely echoed that of the house itself. The front door was opened by a balding man with enormous sideburns, hamster cheeks and a faint whiff of toasted cheese. The frayed cuffs of a once-white shirt poked beneath the arms of his shapeless cardigan. He led the way upstairs to a fusty room piled with boxes, carrier-bags and magazines. Cold slices of half-eaten pizza lay on a greasy paper plate that quivered on the arm of a chair. On the floor, beside the chair, a scree of nail clippings spilled from a fallen jam jar, random sickles, grubby and faintly translucent.

"Would you like to sit down?"

Colin declined hastily and moved further in to the room. As he absorbed more of the junk-laden space around him he saw identical clocks placed in pairs on various items – a tall cabinet, a bookcase stuffed to overflowing – positioned precisely in the middle of each wall.

"They mark the cardinal points," said the man, following his gaze. "That's north above the fireplace. You can work out the rest."

"They all show the same time."

"Isn't that what clocks are supposed to do?"

"But it's the wrong time. They all say half-past twelve."

"They're right twice a day."

"Have they stopped?"

"Of course. They mark the passing of my dear, late mother. She died exactly thirty minutes after midnight in Oxbourne General: the Nightingale Ward. Two years ago next Tuesday. She was seventy-nine."

"I'm sorry. I had no idea."

"I'm the only one here now. The others didn't want to stay. There were four of us with Mother to begin with: Faith, Hope, Charity and me. I'm Bert. Who are you?"

Colin identified himself and repeated his earlier request. "She lived here before you. I heard she was back in town and wondered if she might have come to look at her old home." Anything, he thought, that might provide a clue.

"There was someone, as a matter of fact. A few days ago. I watched her. Through the window. For quite a while. Creeping about, she was. She didn't look well. Unkempt, if you ask me. It's not what you expect in a girl, is it?"

"Did you speak to her?"

"No, no. I just watched. She stood at the entrance to the drive and looked, stared about. Then she came in and…skulked. That's the word for it, skulked…by the laurels. She went on down the side. Between the house and the garage."

"Didn't you ask what she was doing?" asked Colin, a little too quickly.

"No. She, er…she was out of sight at that stage and by the time I came down she'd gone."

That's that, then. Just when I thought I was getting somewhere.

"She must have come back, though," said Bert. "I'll show you."

He followed Bert downstairs, out through the front door and left along a rough brick path crumbling past the side of the garage. Its rotten finial replicated those on the gables of the house. A sign that he had not noticed earlier pointed to the garden flat at the back.

"We used to let it but it's been empty for a while. That's why I didn't bother to lock the door."

The flat was cold and grey, even with the light on, a single shadeless bulb dangling over the fireplace. The place smelled damp and airless. The furniture and pictures had been removed. But here and there were signs of recent occupation. An empty bottle of water; an apple core, heavily discoloured but not yet shrivelled; wrappers from two sausage rolls; a pair of tights screwed up in the corner.

"I didn't see those," said Bert. "Laddered, I shouldn't wonder." He scooped up the tights with a satisfied grunt and stuffed them in his pocket.

Nearing the far wall, a stained mattress, cast adrift in a sea of ill-fitting carpet tiles. A camberwick bedspread was heaped loosely at one end. There was something underneath it. Colin tweaked the bedspread to reveal a pillow, yellowed and misshapen. As he did so, a piece of newspaper swirled to the floor. It was not much more than a scrap: on one side, part of the sports page, by the look of it; on the other, the quick crossword, largely completed in smudgy black biro. The date at the top of the paper was only last week.

"Where's Sanderling?"

"Search me. Never heard of the place."

"It's from the *Sanderling Recorder*. There, by the date. Do you mind if I take it?"

*

The road into town sloped gently down hill with the hint of a curve, past sturdy walls of orange-red brick topped by coping hard in place, past thickening hedges of privet, hawthorn and holly; a road exuding order and comfort, privacy and discretion. He was pained by the contrast with the house he had left a few minutes earlier, a house, it seemed, on the verge of being reclaimed by the closing beech woods, a few bricks beneath a tangle of ivy the only evidence that someone had lived there once.

A cat, curled in a patch of sun on the gravel drive of Comus, the property on the corner of Milton Lane and Oaken Coppice. A ginger cat with a blue collar, partly obscured by fur, reminding him of Toby, his grandmother's companion for many years at her cottage in Somerset. Nutmeg Cottage, he recalled, a white weather-boarded affair, not dissimilar to those he had seen much later in New England, set among fruit trees and retaining the name bestowed by the previous owners, Giles and Eileen Mace.

He had cause to remember that late-summer weekend at the cottage when he was, what, seven, eight? He quickened his pace as he turned into Oaken Coppice. A game of hide-and-seek, the cousins had suggested to him and his sister, Clare. Turfed out of the house for excessive ebullience, they took to the garden, scattering with giggles and yelps as Clare, designated It, was counting up to twenty behind a tree.

The shed. He shuddered at the memory. It was not locked when he came upon it. He stood on tip-toe and prised open the door with slender fingers. He let it creak slowly to a close as he edged round sickle and scythe, clambered over lawn mowers long disused and made himself snug against the shiplap behind the deck chairs leaning at the back.

The door rasped firmly into place, extinguishing the remaining light, for the shed had no windows. He felt secure at first, pleased he had a hiding place that was well concealed. But as the minutes passed the darkness and the silence became oppressive. He began to panic. Where was everyone? He wanted, needed to be found. The shed felt hot and airless. He shifted to get comfortable. It was no good; he had to get out. He stumbled and fumbled past objects blunt and sharp to where he thought the door should be. He pushed and pushed again. It was stuck fast. He kicked and pummelled and called for help, then collapsed sobbing on the floor.

The next he remembered he was in bed, with Toby settled at the end, eyes closed, paws tucked under, purring quietly. They told him later that the latch must have fallen down when the door closed. No one would have shut him in deliberately, would they?

He was sweating as he traipsed into town. He bought a small bottle of water at the Bluebird mini-mart and sat on a bench overlooking the river, swigging periodically. He focused for a while on the stately progress of a pair of swans, making their way towards the three-arched bridge that carried the Bedstead road. On the far side, he caught the rear view of the Nolan brothers, Terry and Frank, lumbering up the hill in jeans and leather jackets, shaven heads shining in the milky sunlight. And then another head, short blond hair, roughly cut. Crossing the bridge from the centre of town, meandering, zigzagging, dodging cars and bicycles. Back turned, the face was away from him, but he was sure it was her. Where had she been, what had she been doing, since she left the flat at Milton Lodge?

He snatched the bottle and ran, along the path, between the bollards and on to the bridge. The figure was making for the old brewery, now converted to offices and studios for local artists. The name he called, once, twice, three times, was lost to the traffic's grumble and roar. It was quieter in the cobbled courtyard of the brewery building. He called again towards the glass door in the far corner, now jerking, juddering to a close. The figure on the other side paused and turned towards him.

Three

Sitting at the kitchen table with coffee and take-away tuna baguette, he thought he had been lucky to get away so lightly. She had taken it in good part, all things considered, seemed amused as much as anything by his stammered apologies and evident discomfort. And, close up, she had looked nothing like Bryony at all. He had better be careful, approaching women on the off-chance like that, running through the streets shouting. Other people might not be so accommodating.

He slipped into his father's study, feeling furtive even though he had the house to himself. It was a small room lined with books from floor to ceiling overlooking Mafeking Avenue, sneaking views of yellow-green hills above and between the houses opposite. He found the motoring atlas of Great Britain, warped and dog-eared from years of use, and took it to the leather-topped desk. He looked up Sanderling in the back. There were several towns of that name scattered over the country south of the Wash. He examined the fragment of newspaper on the desk in front of him. The top two teams in the Boadicea League (Premier Division) were just visible above the tear on one side: Turnstone Wanderers and Dunlin Town. There were a few Turnstones and Dunlins too but only one area where both coincided within a reasonable distance of a place called Sanderling. This put it on the east coast, near the mouth of the River Knot.

He picked up the slim black telephone and dialled a London number.

"Clare Mallory." The voice sounded brisk and efficient.

"It's me, Colin."

"That name rings a bell. I wasn't sure you were still alive. Found a job yet?"

"I've scheduled this week for zero-tasking…"

"Doing fuck all, you mean."

"Language, Miss Mallory. Look, one or two things have happened. Do you remember Bryony Hughes?"

Clare could hardly have forgotten 'that wretched girl', as their mother called her. Others had used stronger language. Bryony was scarcely out of Colin's company at one time, was all he seemed to think about. He practically lived at Milton Lodge. Yet, when it suited her, she had dropped him like a stone, moved on without a backward glance. He had refused to discuss it, stayed in his room and immersed himself in the origins of the First World War.

He filled her in on the previous thirty-six hours.

"The last I heard on the grapevine she was working in a tribute band on a Mediterranean cruise ship. But that was a couple of years ago. Maybe more."

"What about her flat in—? Where was it?"

"South London. Peckham. She gave that up. Everyone went their separate ways. That I do know."

"Well, I think someone's after her. She must be in hiding. Perhaps I should call the police."

"And say what? Aren't you being a bit melodramatic? Anyway, what's it to you? You haven't seen her for years." And would she really want Colin butting in out of the blue after all this time, after the way she had treated him? Even assuming this wasn't all a figment of the over-active imagination from which the family had suffered over the years. Like the time, as a boy, he had denounced Clare's violin teacher as a Russian spy on the strength of a copy of *Pravda* in her shopping bag. Or told the local paper that their neighbour's chinchilla coat was made from the fur of cats she had enticed with poisoned fish. Perhaps he should have been a writer. "If you've got time on your hands there must be something better you could do with it."

"I could go to the town in the newspaper."

"And wander the streets on the off-chance? Be practical."

"If I had a picture, it might help."

"She must have given you one, surely."

"No. Why should she? We saw each other every day."

"What about the plays, then? Haven't you got production photos?"

"Somewhere. But I don't suppose she'd be recognisable underneath the make-up and the wigs. How can I go around with a picture of Lady Macbeth?"

"There's always *Limelight*. You know, that theatrical directory thing with photographs of everyone you've ever heard of and lots you haven't. Try the library, if you must. But what's the point?"

The public library in Church Street was an imposing red brick and sandstone affair displaying the date 'A.D. 1888' high above a weathered coat of arms on the front gable. The clear glass doors opened smoothly of their own accord to admit him to the newly refurbished interior, its cool, clean lines a stark contrast to the High Victorian extravagance outside. Everything had changed. Confronted by racks of DVDs where the fiction used to be, he avoided the hairy assistant at the inquiry desk and took a detour by way of newspapers and periodicals. He lurked behind the shelves of recent acquisitions. He did not want to ask, to increase the risk of being remembered later. As he looked round, he spotted the alphabetical list of subjects on the wall by the lift. Closer inspection revealed that 'Performing Arts' was now in the back room on the first floor. He shunned the lift and took the stairs.

He found what he wanted above circuses and fairgrounds on a high shelf to the left of 'Arts and Crafts'. He took down 'Actresses: H to L', neatly stamped NOT

FOR LOAN, and headed for the quiet area nearby. Most of the tables were occupied by people in attitudes of intense concentration, lost in their own thoughts, present yet absent. There was a tacit understanding that these readers were not to be approached or disturbed.

This atmosphere of self-absorption suited Colin as he wove towards an empty table by a window. It looked over a courtyard bright with mosaics of sea anemones, star fish and other examples of marine life rarely seen in land-locked Oxbourne. The volume in front of him was a few years old but he found Bryony's name in the index and turned to the relevant page.

And there she was! Sharing a double-page spread with two Carolines and a Samantha. She stared straight at him, well-groomed, confident, assured, with the hint of a smile suppressed. He suppressed a wistful smile in turn. This was the Bryony he remembered. Picture taken by Gary at Thespis Studios of Clapham.

'Eyes: blue', it said. A deep blue, flecked with gold, that, in a lyrical moment, he had once compared to lapis lazuli. He coloured at the memory. He glanced at the silent readers and took from his pocket the small packet of razor blades he had lifted from the bathroom cabinet the night before. Slightly rusty but better than being seen to buy them in the town. He removed a blade, slowly, carefully, and held the book close to the vertical as he drew the cutting edge from top to bottom. It took several goes to sever the page completely. It was a neat job.

He folded the liberated sheet in two, the crease

dividing Bryony from one of the Carolines, and secreted it about his person. He was shaking as he returned the blade to the packet and slipped it out of sight. His arm ached and he was drenched in sweat. His shirt clung to his back as he heaved the volume to the shelf. He felt sick and weak with nerves. What if he had been caught? Wasn't defacing library books malicious damage, a criminal act…?

"You have one new message. Message received today at four-fifteen pm."

Blast. Less than ten minutes ago. He pressed one.

"It's me, Col." Bryony! But where, how…? "I tried to see you but they've taken me back." Her voice was strained and shrill. "They don't like people leaving. Sir says it's disloyal." She started talking faster. "I wasn't good enough. That's what they told me. They said I had to work harder until I got it right." Then calmly she said, "I deserve to be punished. I know that. Tonight they will tell me in front of the others. I…" A squeal and the line went dead.

He listened to the message again and again and then once more. That voice, her voice, after all these years. Achingly familiar, disturbingly different. He pressed zero to return the call. It rang but there was no reply. He tried 1471. It was a mobile phone number. Nothing to indicate where she was. He wrote down the number and pressed three to return the call by that route. A gentle hiss, then silence.

His thoughts were racing: elated, concerned, confused.

She was being held against her will. That much was clear. Why else had she tried to escape? But from what or whom? Some kind of group or sect, with this 'Sir' as its leader? How on earth had she got caught up in that? Her distress was all too evident. Yet there was an underlying matter-of-factness, an acceptance of whatever was in store for her that he found even more unsettling.

The *Limelight* entry gave her agent's name and contact details. A bit old but worth a try. He rang the number.

"Bryony Hughes? Well may you ask. We'd very much like to know where she is ourselves. Never answers calls or correspondence. We've decided to take her off the books."

The agent parted with Bryony's own contact details without too much fuss but they plainly related to her old Peckham flat. She could hardly expect work to be put her way if she did not keep them up-to-date. Maybe that was the point: she was being held captive somewhere and could not keep her agent in touch. And yet she had been able to phone him, Colin, even if the call had been cut short.

He dredged from his memory a clutch of contemporaries from St George's and struggled to recall where they had lived. The phone book yielded numbers but calls were no more productive. One had moved, one was abroad, a third had just got back from work but knew nothing of Bryony's current whereabouts.

There was only one option left.

Four

"We are now approaching Sanderling. Would customers please alight from the front four coaches only as this station has a short platform."

Colin slid a hand inside his jacket pocket as he walked from the station towards the centre of the town. It was still there, warm and safe next to his book. Another slim volume of short stories bought at the Harvard Book Store, this time by Tobias Wolff. He seemed incapable of concentrating on anything longer just at the moment.

He had cut her picture from the page last night, trimmed it carefully with the kitchen scissors, and covered it with some sticky-backed plastic he had found in the middle drawer of the dresser. Picture and sketch rested against a couple of empty bottles of burgundy he meant to replace before his parents got back. The contrast was painful. And yet the man had said she looked worse 'in the flesh'. Why he had bothered to tone down the sketch was unclear. It was hardly flattering as it was and he had not expected her to take it in any event. Colin knew there was something he had meant to ask the man but he could not remember what it was. The space outside the shop had been empty when he went back to the square on Saturday, snaking through side streets to avoid the mêlée of the market. Hatchet Face in the café, pausing for a nanosecond with damp cloth in one hand and trigger spray in the other, said she had only noticed the man there once, the day Colin had seen him himself.

Tight brick terraces gave way to spacious villas as Station Road turned into Mallard Drive, all stucco and blossom and wrought-iron balconies. Books, more books, a grand piano, a flickering computer screen. No net curtains here to keep out prying eyes. It was good to be outside. Sitting by the window had helped, pushing through damp woods and fields, ghostly tunnels, empty platforms.

He paused when he came to the high street, consulted the map he had printed off in the early hours, and turned right. The route to the theatre, lined almost entirely with estate agents, fish restaurants and charity shops, curved gently in the direction of the old harbour. Above the garish fascias were remnants of an older town, of proportion and restraint, cold grey slate against a sullen sky.

The Darlington Theatre, named in honour of the well-known actor-manager Sir Norbert Darlington, had opened to much acclaim in the 1960s, an event graced by minor royalty and much enhanced by the presence of the late Sir Norbert himself. Built to provide a permanent home for the Sanderling Rep, the theatre closed in 1999 after a decade of financial troubles culminating in the loss of its grant from the district council. The award-winning building, erected on the site of the old Rex Cinema, now lay in darkness, its future unresolved as the arguments continued. This much Colin knew from the website of the Theatres Preservation Trust.

He peered through the gaps between posters stuck firmly to the plate glass windows. The empty foyer was stacked high with folding chairs, its worn brown carpet strewn with lengths of cable, empty crisp packets, letters that would never be read, let alone answered. The pale concrete walls, textured like planks of wood, matched their grim counterparts outside.

So much for regional theatre, he thought. It wasn't this brought Bryony here. We were still at school when it closed.

He had found no recent reference to the Sanderling Rep. Had that at least survived the demise of the Darlington, found another base? Someone must know.

The tourist office was a little further down the high street, a forlorn attempt to uphold the remaining dignity of the frontage between the Happy Times noodle bar and My Plaice restaurant and take-away.

"The Rep bit the dust in the 1980s, I fear." This from the woman, cashmere and pearls, sitting behind a small square desk aching with leaflets, maps and guides.

"I was at the last night. *Our Town*. Thornton Wilder. Do you know it?"

Colin mumbled and shook his head.

"The place staggered on for another ten years or so, playing host to touring companies mostly. Here today, gone tomorrow. No local connection or interest in the community. A week in the summer for the Sanderling Operatic and that was it. Then the council pulled the plug. They'd like to knock it down but it's Grade II listed. Ha!"

"So what happens now? Isn't there any theatrical activity in the town at all?"

With a flourish, the woman produced a leaflet out of nowhere, in the manner of a conjuror. "The Sanderling Arts and Leisure Centre. This is the spring programme. The building's on the harbour front. Looks like a gigantic upturned boat." She leaned forward, looked hastily to left and right, and added in a half-whisper, "I recommend the crab sandwiches in the Samphire café on the top floor." What prompted this confidential approach was unclear: there was no one else in the tourist office at all.

'An Evening of Magic and Mirth with Mr Mussels', 'What a Hoot! Quips and Capers at the Cockles Comedy Club', 'A Mozart Medley with the Turnstone Consort'. This was not promising. Colin worked his way through the leaflet from back to front. 'Fifty Years A Shucker: Arnold Smith Reveals All (with slides)'. 'Oompah! Oompah! Have a Rousing Time with the

Sanderling Scouts Brass Ensemble'. Not promising at all.

He finished his crab sandwich and stared out of the café window, across the gently dipping boats in the harbour, over the sharp roofs of black-boarded fishermen's huts, past timber groynes stepping down the yellow-grey beach towards the distant sea, a thin strip of pewter merging with the sky. Could she really be here, behind some unassuming façade, held against her will?

'Django Brazil and his Fascinating Rhythm Boys', 'Don't Drop It! Juggling workshops for the over tens'. This was hopeless. Perhaps the winter programme might give a clue about what had brought her to Sanderling. She could hardly perform in public now if she was shut away somewhere, but how long had she been out of circulation? He wished he had thought to ask the agent when she had last heard from Bryony.

He drained his cup, the dregs of coffee bitter and cold, and made his way through the largely empty café and down the wooden stairs. At the bottom, he glanced idly at the notice board he had shot past on his way up. There, in the middle, between the flyer for the Charity Knitathon and a postcard for the forthcoming exhibition of new work by local artist Lucy Potter, a small but colourful poster, not much more than a handbill. 'PAYING A WELCOME RETURN VISIT TO SANDERLING: The Enigma Theatre Company presents *The Tempest* by William Shakespeare.' Performances next week at the Church Hall, Victoria Road.

He tried the number given for enquiries and booking tickets. A recorded message told him that the box office was closed for another two hours. He snapped his phone shut with frustration. He couldn't just sit around and wait. He had to get on, make some progress. At least he could see if there was anyone at the hall who knew something about the company. He pulled the map from his pocket and found Victoria Road, accessible by way of the high street and Albert Terrace.

The church hall was a brick and pebbledash structure, set well back from the road in landscaped grounds, with large double doors at the front and high semi-circular windows at the sides. There was no church anywhere near it. Posters for *The Tempest* were neatly pinned to the doors at regular intervals. Colin turned the shiny brass handle. The doors shuddered and squeaked but did not open. He tried again. And again. And again. The noise turned heads in Victoria Road.

"I think they're locked," called a man bowling past in yachting cap and cream flannels.

Colin acknowledged his helpful assessment and sank to a bench by a bed of wallflowers and forget-me-nots. He was sweating and breathing heavily. He heard footsteps from the path at the side of the hall. Now what? He was approached by a tallish man with a full head of grey hair, a denim suit, and a relaxed demeanour.

" '*Hast thou, spirit, / Perform'd to point the tempest that I bade thee?*' Jolly good sound effects. Your thunder claps would wake the dead. I sense that you were trying to gain entry. Would that your enthusiasm were more widely shared by the denizens of Sanderling."

"Sorry, I…"

"Think nothing of it. I'm Ken Westow, by the way." He thrust a hand in Colin's direction. It was disconcertingly soft and had a flowery fragrance that he could not place. "General manager of the Enigma and director of this 'ere play. I'm casing the joint before the company arrive from Croydon. There's another door down the side, you know. Are you after tickets?"

"I'm trying to find a young actress…"

"Aren't we all, dear. I admire your candour. Not everyone would be so direct."

"No, I mean a particular actress."

"And discriminating, too. Very commendable."

"She's someone I know. Or used to. I've lost touch with her. I've heard she's in Sanderling but I don't have her address. I wondered if anyone had come across her or knew where she was."

"What is she called, this particular actress?" asked Ken, sliding onto the bench beside him and draping an arm over the back.

"Er, Bryony Hughes," said Colin, edging towards the corner.

"Bryony Hughes. It's not ringing bells, I'm afraid."

"Perhaps you might recognise her." He drew the *Limelight* picture from his inside pocket.

"Well, well, well. I may forget a name but I never forget a face. Nice-looking girl."

"What? You've seen her?" said Colin, sitting up straight.

"Yes, but not recently. She was in our production of…what was it? So many plays, so many plays. *Much Ado*. That's right. It's coming back to me now. A year or so ago. She played Hero, Leonato's daughter. The victim of a strange deceit."

"I know it."

"And very good she was too. It was a successful tour. The run ended here…"

"In Sanderling?"

"In this very 'all. She left during the party and I haven't seen her since. A bit abrupt, to put it mildly. I don't think she said goodbye to anyone. A few people were pretty upset about that."

"Left to do what?"

"I've no idea. I don't think she had anything else lined up."

"Was there anything odd about the last night – or about Bryony before she went off?"

"Not that I recall. Apart from being a full house. That's unusual in itself. Oh, and the audience was graced by the presence of Howard Desmond and his lovely wife, Celerity Box."

"Who?"

"A bit before your time, perhaps. They were a famous acting couple but well past their sell-by date. To be honest, I thought they were dead. I doubt that many others would have recognised them." Ken looked at his watch. "D'you have time for a quick one? I'll just go and lock the side door."

*

They sat at a table in the garden of the Sailor's Retreat, a quiet pub on the corner of Victoria Road and Albert Terrace. Ken's pint of Curate's Winkle glowed amber in the late afternoon sun. Colin thought it prudent to stick to coffee. It was a long way back to Oxbourne in any case.

"He was never an actor of the first rank," said Ken. "But he was a good second division player. A stalwart of weekly rep. Took over from Stamford Brook at Hornchurch for a while. That's where I saw first saw him, as Abanazer in *Aladdin*, sometime in the early 'sixties. Frightened the life out of me. "

"You were still at school?"

"I certainly was. Hadn't yet taken my eleven plus."

Colin looked blank.

"Anyway, he and Celerity B had a string of successes in the West End in totally forgettable plays. I used to see their pictures in *Curtain Up!* It was one of the theatre mags. Hasn't existed for years."

"And then?"

"He wangled a job as director at the late lamented Sanderling Rep. Tried to redeem his reputation as a serious actor with forays into the classics. Mostly vehicles for him and his good lady wife, if you ask me. Eventually, the Rep folded and it was downhill all the way. A few character parts. The odd bit of telly. Eventually, the phone stops ringing for good. Comes to us all, in the end."

"So they retired round here?"

"Not a clue," said Ken, with an affected shrug. "I expect they were passing through, like thousands of others with a craving for a shovelful of shellfish before their cream teas. They're probably tucked up in a nursing home somewhere. I haven't seen any obituaries."

Five

Colin turned over in the half-light and pulled the quilt towards him. A large black-and-white poster of Brooklyn Bridge loomed menacingly above. It had been a job getting the thing back on the plane and even worse trying to extricate it from its cardboard tube without causing the damage the tube was designed to prevent.

Beyond the door and down the stairs he could hear the clanking and whining of Mrs Nolan at work. He had forgotten that she would be early at number twenty-six this week so she could attend a family funeral on Friday somewhere on the outskirts of Liverpool.

He reached blindly for the glass of water on his bedside cabinet. He started as something rough and ridged came to fingertip. It was the oyster shell he had picked up and slipped in his pocket in his rush to Sanderling station after the drink with Ken. He had liked the shape and the texture and the pleasing sharpness of its uneven edges. It could do some damage in the wrong hands.

He turned and turned again. It was no good. He was never going to get back to sleep with that racket. He slid out of bed, lifted his dressing gown from the back of the door and shambled towards the window. Through a gap in the curtains, a sliver of glass, stippled with rain. He widened the gap tentatively. A fox on the lawn, frozen in mid-lope, stared up at him with sad eyes. A vulpine arrangement in russet and grey.

He stepped over one pile of books and then another and dropped onto a wicker chair. He picked up a Boston Red Sox cap, souvenir of his only visit to Fenway Park, and twirled it half-heartedly in his right hand before propelling it towards the bed. It fell well short of the target.

He was disappointed that he did not have more to show for his trip to Sanderling, though what he had expected he was not sure. He had only shown Bryony's picture to one person. In the event, his courage had failed him. He couldn't assail people on the off-chance. He needed more to go on. Admittedly, Ken Westow had seen her, or so he said. But not recently. 'A year or so ago.' Maybe he should have pressed Ken to be more precise on timing. A bit odd that he did not spark on the name straightaway considering she had had a decent part in one of his own productions. He wondered about Ken's relaxed approach and relentless affability: was he always like that or was he stringing him along for some reason?

Either way, what on earth had Bryony been doing in the town since her abrupt departure from the Enigma? Was she actually there at all? She had not said where she was when she left her message. It all rested on a scrap of newspaper. But if she had made her way to Oxbourne from Sanderling she had obviously been taken back there. Whoever 'they' were must therefore have been in Oxbourne themselves only a week or two before. The thought was unsettling. How did they know where she was or manage to spirit her away without anyone noticing? He needed to see Bert again in case there was something else, anything, to point him in the right direction.

Mrs Nolan was returning the vacuum cleaner to the cupboard under the stairs when Colin plodded down, newly showered and shaved.

"Good morning, your lordship. Or should I say good afternoon? Did I wake you up?"

"No. I was just thinking," he said, heading for the kitchen.

"More thinking? Not another of your brown days, is it?"

"They're Fridays. Today's Tuesday, isn't it?"

"It is."

"Tuesdays are green."

"Here we go again."

"I told you words had colours."

"Like pigs have wings. Grass-green, is it? Or more like moss?"

"Darker than moss. It's what my father calls British racing green."

"*Darker than Moss*," said Mrs Nolan distantly. She enunciated each word clearly. "*Darker than Moss*. That takes me back."

"To what?"

"More years than I care to remember. I must have been younger than you are when I saw it up in town. It was a play I was taken to see by a gentleman friend, with Howard Desmond and Celery Box."

"Would that perhaps be *Celerity* Box?"

"It would, now I come to think of it. I'm surprised you've heard of her. They must be six feet under by now, the pair of them. I put the magazines on the dresser, by the rock cakes. Miss Campion brought round the bag while you were in bed."

The magazines were copies of *The Dragon*, the journal of St George's School, Oxbourne. Colin had a complete run from his seven years there, the earlier ones with plain blue covers, the later enlivened with bold but derivative examples of sixth-form art work. He had taken them down the night before from the highest shelf of the cupboard in his bedroom. They had lain there undisturbed while he had been away.

At the kitchen table he wiped the dust off the top copy with a chequered dish cloth that was waiting to be washed. He flicked through the magazine, indifferent to the achievements of St George's athletes, the opening of the science block, news of Old Georgians. Had he cared once? He found drama. Just the Lower School production of *The Fire Raisers*. Of course, the others had had exams in the summer term.

He turned to older issues. Pictures of productions past flared in the kitchen spots. Pictures of him and Bryony, together or alone, embedded in the fulsome reviews of critics identified only by initials. Here he was as Creon in epaulettes and frogging ('a forceful and confident performance'), with Bryony sitting by herself ('intense and assured as the tragic heroine Antigone'). There, steadfast as Sir Thomas More ('outstanding…truly a man for all seasons') trying to explain to his wife Alice ('played with dignity and unaffected simplicity').

And so on. How young she seemed, how young they both seemed, beneath the veneer of disguise and false maturity. How on earth had they mastered those parts, learned the lines, found the time and the energy? It was puzzling that she had made so little impact on the wider world, an oddity reinforced by Ken Westow's positive comments about her performance as Hero. 'I wasn't good enough. That's what they told me.'

People said at the time that he too should go into the business. People who claimed to know, aging cronies of various producers having loose associations with the West End stage, present and past. But what was the point? Doing a few school plays was one thing. Spending half his life pretending to be other people was quite another, spouting words put into his mouth, delivering performances both repetitious and ephemeral, forgotten before the audience got home. In any case, he could so easily have sunk without trace, much like Bryony, and joined the ranks of part-time waiters and barmen. What was it Ken had said? 'Eventually, the phone stops ringing for good. Comes to us all, in the end.'

He flicked through the last magazines in the now disordered pile. Bryony 'utterly charming' as Lydia Languish in *The Rivals*. And his own final appearance: *Hamlet* relatively uncut: Colin Mallory as the prince himself. 'A mature and well-judged interpretation rarely seen on the school stage…a gem of a performance.' With Bryony as Ophelia, of course. She had developed a good line in stage madness.

He took the direct route to Milton Lane, avoiding the dripping trees and puddled paths of the woods. The wet slates of the Lodge shone painfully in the sun breaking through the thinning cloud, pale-grey stained by patches of the intensest blue.

'Not enough to make a pair of sailor's trousers,' he found himself saying, just as his mother always said and her mother before her. He wondered where his parents were now. Wyoming, was it, or up to Missoula, Montana, to seek out distant cousins?

He made for the porch, stepped over the sodden newspaper disintegrating just inside, and stabbed the grubby bell push. High in the hall the bell grumbled quietly, hissed and went dead. There was no other sound from within. He grasped the big black knocker, moulded in the shape of a diving dolphin, and rammed it hard against the metal plate beneath. Once, twice, three times.

The noise, both dull and piercing, reverberated throughout the house. And then another noise, shuffling and mumbling and tugging of bolts.

"All right, all right. I'm coming."

The door was drawn slowly inwards by the thick and hairy hand of Bert. The rest of the man appeared in stages, clothing in disarray, belt dangling. He was not in good humour.

"Loud enough to wake the dead," he muttered. "What do you want this time? I told you before…oh, it's you."

"Who did you think it was?"

"Just someone. A persistent caller, you might say. What can I do for you? Did you find your friend?"

"That's why I'm here. Could we…?"

The curtains in the upstairs room were still closed. The air was warm and stale and faintly humid. A standard lamp with a parchment shade lit Bert's chair but not much else. The absence of greasy plate and cold sliced pizza made it no more appealing.

Bert parted the curtains roughly and fastened his belt.

"So you went to that place, did you? The one in the paper?"

"Sanderling, yes," said Colin, "but…but no luck. I'm not sure what I expected to find, really." He felt uneasy about mentioning Bryony's call or his encounter with Ken Westow. "I was wondering whether you saw or heard anything when she left the garden flat."

"I don't know when she left it. I didn't even know she'd stayed there until after she'd gone."

"She may not have left voluntarily. There could have been a struggle. Did you see anyone else hanging around?"

"Kidnapping, eh? In Oxbourne? Sounds a bit unlikely. How would they have known where to find her?"

A good point, thought Colin. A very good point. Perhaps they had followed her from town. "Nothing parked outside?" he put in weakly.

"Nothing that I remember. Apart from a dark blue van. That was there when I went shopping one time but not when I came back. Could have been anything."

"I suppose so." This was getting nowhere. Even if Bryony had been taken while Bert was out that shed no light on where she was now. He was no further forward.

He wondered what Bert did all day, closeted in this sordid room with piles of junk and clocks that did not work. If anything, the bags and boxes had encroached even further on the shabby green carpet in the short time since he was here before.

A violent trumpeting brought him sharply back to focus. "Better out than in," said Bert, fanning the area behind him with a well-thumbed catalogue of 'Naughty but Nice', plucked with surprising speed from a heap beside his chair. "Shan't be a mo'," he said, handing the catalogue to Colin and leaving the room at the double.

Colin retreated to safer parts and glanced with little interest at the dismal document, published by a chain of adult shops based in East Anglia and lavishly illustrated in colour. Several pages had been torn out, folded in half lengthways and inserted at the back of the catalogue, undislodged by Bert's brief but frantic fanning. There was no theme or pattern to the removal that he could see.

No sign of Bert. He placed the catalogue beside a pair of clocks on the mantelpiece, took a deep breath and made quickly for the door. Exhaling on the landing, he went not down the stairs to the hall but along a corridor he used to know. Past one panelled door, then another. He took the handle of the third gently in his hand and turned.

This used to be Bryony's room. But memories of posters, make-up and innumerable soft toys were rapidly dispelled by what he saw now. The gloomy space, curtains drawn, appeared to be empty but for a large mahogany table in the middle crammed with framed photographs of women, or possibly one woman at various stages of her life. They were arranged around a large and lighted candle, guttering quietly and casting long shadows across the floor.

As his eyes adjusted, he saw a bag leaning against the far wall facing the door. It was a red plastic bag with another frame sticking out of the top. He went forward to have a closer look. What the…? Printed on the bag the words: 'Fun Fashions, 98 High Street, Sanderling'. As he drew the frame slowly from the bag, a face rose to meet him. It was a sketch of the woman occupying the table in the centre of the room.

"Exploring, are we?"

He wheeled round in fright. "I was…I was just filling

in time. I knew this room once. Years ago. It was Bryony's."

"Well, I know it as my late mother's bedroom. I don't care for violation of the sanctum."

"Sorry. Is this…?" Colin nodded towards the sketch he was slipping back into the bag.

"It is. A recent acquisition, I am happy to say."

"I thought your mother died a couple of years ago."

"And so she did. This was drawn from a photograph. The man said it made a change from dogs and cats."

"And the bag? It comes from Sanderling."

"Never been there. Don't know the place at all. I must have picked it up in the flat after your friend went."

And left the other rubbish? Like pigs have wings, as Mrs Nolan would say. But what else did he have to go on? Colin left the house more confused than ever by the malodorous flatulist of Milton Lane.

Six

Colin dribbled the last of the wine into his glass, polished it off in one gulp and lay back on the settee with a copy of that week's television guide resting on his chest. Within moments he was asleep.

He found himself in a long corridor, pale and putty-coloured, lit by skylights set at intervals in the ceiling. On both sides, identical doors without handles alternated with pictures screwed face down to the walls. The whole had a textured, grainy feel, as if he were viewing it through gauze or mesh.

He was wearing doublet and hose and hobnail boots yet no sound emerged as he strode along the bare floorboards. The corridor was cool and tranquil and calm. He knew he was making for something at the end but the quicker he walked the further away it became. He started to run. His goal receded with equal speed. He ran faster and faster; the corridor stretched into infinity. He stopped, breathing heavily, and put a hand against a door for support. It opened and he fell inside a windowless room illuminated by a gigantic candle in a brass holder. Men in red baseball caps, sitting on folding stools, were arranged around it in a semi-circle with their backs to the door. They started talking loudly without turning round.

"Ah, the Lorelei. Beautiful but deadly."

"It's not what you expect in a girl, is it?"

"I recommend the crab sandwiches."

"Enjoy."

"I'm here on a Friday."

"Found a job yet?"

The hubbub ceased as abruptly as it had started. The men stood up in unison, folded their stools and left the room through a door on the far side. Each was clutching a pair of garden shears. In their place Colin saw a pile of hair, roughly cut. It shone like gold in the light of the candle.

And now another man, his face hidden in shadows in a corner of the room. " '*Hast thou spirit,/Perform'd to point the tempest that I bade thee?*' Use the bellows." Colin struggled to pick up the enormous leather bellows that had appeared in front of him. He began to work them furiously. A wind got up that grew rapidly in strength and blew the hair into the darkness. The ceiling became the sky and it started to rain, harder and harder. The room began to flood. The candle was the mast of a ship with a lantern at the top. He was on deck wearing oil skins and a sou'wester. The water rose and flowed into the corridor that was now a river lined with weeping willows. He could see something floating in the water by the far bank. It was a young woman in a white dress, adorned with flowers. As he tried to grab one of her raised arms she flipped over and back again. She was an old woman, wearing a maid's uniform, bright red lipstick and turquoise eye shadow. Her eyes opened. "I'm Bert's mother," she said. "Naughty but nice." Her cackling, shrill, mirthless, penetrating.

He woke with a start, feeling weak and thick-headed. He scrabbled for the phone, lifted the receiver and managed one word. "Hallo."

"I thought I ought to come and see you," said Clare. She had her brother's slim build and dark brown hair. It was cut short in a sensible, practical style. "You sounded in a right state on the phone this morning." She slammed the front door, marched into the kitchen and sat down. Colin shuffled behind her.

"I'd only just woken up. I wasn't entirely with it."

"You're telling me. On the booze again, I suppose. Is there anything left in the cellar? This place is a tip. You haven't been upsetting Mrs Nolan, have you?"

"I was just about to clear it up. And get a replacement case or two. I can order it on line. There's no hurry."

"I don't know what you do all day. You don't seem to be focusing on anything, just drifting. How did you manage to get a *summa cum laude*, or whatever it was, at Harvard?"

"It takes time to adjust. And I've been distracted by this Bryony business. I'd almost forgotten her while I was away but this is bringing everything back."

"You were pretty cut up at the time."

"She made it clear she wanted to go in a different direction. There was no part for me. I did mean to keep in touch but the longer I left it the more difficult it became. You know how it is. And she moved away in any case."

"There was her parents' funeral after the car crash. She was in Oxbourne for that. So was I."

"I couldn't have flown back, not then."

"You could have written. I had her new address, the one in Peckham."

"I suppose so. Well, I'm trying to make up for it now. 'Trying' being the operative word. I'm getting nowhere." He mentioned Bert and the carrier bag. "At least the Hughes can't see the state the place is in now."

"I wonder why the Bert clan bought it in the first place or left him to fester there by himself. It's hardly an investment if it's falling about his ears."

"No idea." And there's another thing that's been puzzling me, he thought. What did Bryony do with the money she got from sale of the house? Why waste her time earning a pittance with touring companies or tribute bands or whatever it was she was doing before she disappeared?

Clare glanced at the open copies of *The Dragon* spread over the table, closed each in turn, and piled them neatly in one corner in date order. She sat back and looked pensive. She cradled a mug of coffee in her hands.

"You know, you weren't a bad actor," she said.

"Thank you kindly, Miss Mallory. Much appreciated, I'm sure."

"I mean it. Have you read these reviews? People used to say you were better than Bryony."

"Ah, the benchmark of success. Or should I say Touchstone? Much good did it do her. What makes you think I'd have had any more luck in the real world beyond St George's?"

"I didn't say do it professionally."

"What, then? I can't see the point. All that effort and nothing to show for it afterwards, except a few production photographs. Your performance just melts into thin air. It's all so…ephemeral, insubstantial. Creating a role in a play isn't like painting a picture or writing a book or recording a CD. At least they have some degree of permanence."

"Verging on the articulate, young Colin. Almost convincing. Perhaps you should be a barrister, like me."

"I don't know what I want. But I'll know it when I see it."

It was in the hall when he got back from seeing Clare off at the station. Not on the mat but a little beyond, a plain buff rectangle against the blues and oranges of the Turkish carpet. His first instinct was to straighten the envelope, to relate its shape and position more satisfactorily to the abstract design running along the carpet's border. But he scooped the envelope up and took it into the kitchen, turning it over as he went. There was no name or address on the envelope and nothing to indicate who it was from. Was it for him, his parents or the people next door? It was probably another boring circular from the Residents' Association about overhanging branches, replacement windows, or the state of the roads.

He took a knife from the kitchen drawer and ran it swiftly along the flap. The envelope gaped to reveal two others inside, not buff themselves but the sort of chalky blue that his grandmother used to use for her letters at Christmas. He tumbled them onto the work surface and took them over to the table. Neither envelope was sealed.

From one, he removed a rectangle of thin, white cardboard. It was about the size of a postcard. A curl of hair – blond, golden – was cellotaped to it. From the other, he unfolded a piece of A4 paper. It was a photograph of himself, leaving the café at Sanderling Leisure Centre. Some words were printed neatly in block capitals underneath:

> '*The crows and choughs that wing the midway air*
> *Show scarce so gross as beetles; half way down*
> *Hangs one that gathers samphire, dreadful trade!*'

He ran to the front door, opened it with a bang and took the steps two at a time. Mafeking Avenue was deserted, the only noise that of his own breathing. What he had expected to see he had no idea since the envelope had clearly been propelled through the letter box while he was out. He just felt the need to do something but the action merely underlined his own sense of impotence.

He sat down heavily at the kitchen table and looked again at the objects lying there. The hair was presumably Bryony's or intended to represent it. As for the photograph of him leaving the Samphire café... . Someone had no doubt enjoyed the joke. He dimly recalled the lines from *King Lear* that he had read, but not performed, at St George's.

So they knew he was looking for her. Was he being encouraged or warned off or merely taunted? How did they know he was going to be in Sanderling that day? He shuddered at the thought that he was being watched, photographed. And someone had been to the house here in Oxbourne within the last hour or so.

Seven

---

*H*e did not linger when he arrived at Sanderling. He knew the way to the high street. As he strode along pavements washed by early morning rain, he rehearsed what he would say when he reached number ninety-eight.

But Fun Fashions was no longer there. He kicked an empty beer can in frustration, turning heads as it bounced and clattered into the road. So much for checking the website of the Sanderling Chamber of Commerce, he thought. He couldn't even rely on that.

The premises were now occupied by the Lobster Pot café and sandwich bar. A sign on the glass door said 'CLOSED' but he could see a figure moving inside. He pushed the door roughly and went in.

"We're closed," shrilled a small woman with a red face, white shirt and blue overalls. She raised her mop like a flail and lashed the floor.

"Yes, I…"

"Have you brought the baps?" came a thin voice from a dark corner towards the back. "We're clean out of wholemeal."

"No, I…"

"You'll have to come back later, my love," purred a raven-haired woman with an assertive cleavage, lightly dusted with freckles. She had just appeared through a door at the side.

"I'm looking for Fun Fashions. I thought it was here."

"Like a bit of fun, do you?"

"Er…"

"Women's clothes your thing, are they?"

"I just…"

"Each to his own, I say."

"Is it…?"

"They've moved to Old Harbour Street. Halfway down on the right. Don't think they do your size, though."

He left the café to the thwack of a mop and gales of high-pitched laughter. He was much the same colour as the plastic lobster cringing on the counter.

His route took him past the Darlington Theatre, a dull grey box under a dull grey sky, looking even more forlorn than the last time he had seen it. Further on, the road divided and flowed either side of the Crown and Sea Horse, an imposing Victorian edifice with patterned brickwork like a Fair Isle sweater. Colin took the right fork down Old Harbour Street. Fun Fashions had fetched up in a weather-boarded building on a corner next to Spinnakers marine chandlery. Even in the weak sun that had just emerged the newly painted exterior of Fun Fashions was painfully white. Inside, the effect was worse, blanched walls and carpet dazzling in the spots.

He wiped his feet vigorously on the coconut matting before penetrating the brightness. The rasping raised the heads of customers drawing hangers slowly across gleaming chrome rails.

"Can I help you?" asked a tanned woman, no longer young. She laid a hand on one hip of her well-cut trousers.

Colin gulped and cleared his throat. "I was…I was wondering if you'd seen a friend of mine." He produced Bryony's picture from his inside pocket and showed it to her.

"No," she said, with little pause for reflection. "I don't think so. I'd remember a pretty girl like that."

"She may have changed a bit. Cut her hair."

"What a shame. Why should I have seen her?"

"She may have been a customer of yours. She had a carrier bag with the address of your old shop. A red bag."

"A *red* bag?" The woman took a step back. "We stopped using *those* three years ago."

"She wasn't in Sanderling then, as far as I know. I only saw the bag the day before yesterday. It looked fairly new."

A shorter woman appeared through curtains hanging like shrouds in an opening to the side. She had hennaed hair and an olive-green dress.

"We chucked out a whole load of the old bags when we left number ninety-eight," she said. Her chunky amber bracelets rattled as she moved. "We found them in a box at the back of the store room. They were unused: pristine, you might say."

"What happened to them?"

"We gave them to one of the charity shops in the high street. I can't remember which, offhand."

"So your friend probably got the bag from there and not from us at all," said the tanned woman, sniffily. She left him to deal with a customer trying to attract her attention from the entrance to the changing rooms.

The other woman rattled through the curtains and produced a shiny red bag, identical to the one he had seen at Bert's. "This is the very last bag." It slipped from her fingers and lay on the carpet like blood on freshly fallen snow. Colin felt a frisson of excitement, of anticipation, as he stooped to pick it up.

He rejected the Samphire café in favour of the Mermaid, a tile-hung pub standing by itself close to the beach. It was some distance from the town centre. For some reason that made it feel safer, made *him* feel safer. He knew it was not logical: if they could watch him before, they could watch him again. There was no real difference between being followed to one place and being followed to another. Perhaps he had been tracked ever since he arrived in Sanderling. On the other hand, from his position near the door to the lounge bar, he could at least see who came and went and, being by a window, he had a view of those outside.

After a couple of pints of Curate's Winkle and a plate of plaice and chips he began to relax. He would happily have stayed there but time was passing. Charity shops had an inconvenient habit of closing early as he knew from rummaging in those in Oxbourne. And he had counted over a dozen in the high street alone.

After a while, he developed a routine involving the increasingly dog-eared picture of Bryony and the increasingly battered carrier bag. The outcome was invariably the same: sucking of teeth, shaking of heads, expressions of sympathy and support. Some appeared to find his mission touching, others frankly odd. A few recoiled at sight of the carrier bag, recalling attempts by Fun Fashions to offload dozens of the things on them several months before.

By late afternoon, he had given up. One or two charity shops he had missed were now in darkness. He shuffled down an alley, crooked and cobbled, thinking about what to do next. Turning a corner, he was confronted by the head of a donkey in a window in front of him. His first, dazed thought was that it was his own reflection, that he had been transformed like Bottom the weaver. It was a punishment for the folly of his futile and fruitless expedition, a warning from those who held Bryony captive to weaken his resolve.

'I see their knavery: this is to make an ass of me;
to fright me, if they could. But I will not stir

from this place, do what they can: I will walk up and down here, and I will sing, that they shall hear I am not afraid.'

He saw that it was a poster, an advertisement for the Sanderling and District Donkey Welfare League, seeking funds for the rescue and rehabilitation of ill-treated and abandoned animals.

The window was cluttered with spidery bric-a-brac, yellowing paperbacks and toppled donkeys made of straw. He peered through the grimy glass. He made out movement in the murk within. Pushing the door with unnecessary force, he fell into the shop and came to rest at the feet of a sensibly shod woman wearing an overcoat of Harris tweed. She had a weather-beaten face and short brown hair. The donkey brooch on her lapel gleamed intermittently in the fitful light of a fluorescent tube that had but a short time to live.

"Welcome, welcome. Good to have a return customer."

"I don't think we've…"

"No, no. I rotate with Daphne Shepherd and Norman Tonsley. We take it in turns on the bridge."

"But why do you…?"

"The bag, boy, the bag." She made it sound the most obvious thing in the world. "It's what we use. A job lot from Fun Fashions. They'll last us for years at the present rate."

Colin cut to the chase. A practised hand went inside his jacket. "Have you seen this girl? She's a friend of mine."

"Indeed I have. Indeed I have."

"Are you sure?" His heart leapt. "She may have cut her hair short."

"Not when I've seen her. Long and flowing. Like Rapunzel."

"You've seen her more than once?"

"Two or three times, I'd say. Sometimes with that other one."

"What other one?"

"The other girl. Mousy little thing. Wearing the same tracksuit, though."

Colin looked blank.

"Your friend always wears a maroon tracksuit. I can't think why. It's a most unflattering colour."

"What sort of things does she buy?"

"Clothes, mostly." She waved in the direction of another room that he had not noticed in the gloom. "Invariably leaves sand on the floor. I take a stiff brush to it, pronto."

"Sand?"

"She must have been on the beach. I daresay she was collecting shells or bits of coloured glass. People do, you know."

The conversation was reaching a natural conclusion. He had one more question.

"Have you seen her recently?"

"A couple of weeks ago, perhaps. Possibly longer. Of course, she may have been in when Daphne or Norman were at the helm."

She coughed and looked towards a collection box

on the counter. Colin flushed and put a hand in his pocket.

The sky was indigo, smudged with grey. The last train to connect with one to Oxbourne had long since departed. He regretted, briefly, that he had never got round to taking his driving test; his parents' Rover festered unused in the garage at twenty-six Mafeking Avenue.

He had passed B and Bs declaring vacancies on his way from the station: Smugglers' Rest, Neptune's Locker, Sea Holly House. Salubrious, no doubt, but dull. He preferred to risk the Mermaid, in whose window he had spotted at lunchtime a small, grubby card claiming that rooms were available.

The public bar was deserted when Colin entered, deserted but for the red-faced man gyrating by the till at the far end. He was juggling scotch eggs and whistling the 'Dambusters March'. An egg crashed to the floor, bounced and rolled across the room.

"The dam's held," he said, tweaking nose between thumb and forefinger. "I'll draw the flak while you…" He faltered as Colin came into view. "Not to worry," he said, retrieving the egg and moulding it roughly back to shape. "All hygienically wrapped in the very finest hand-knitted cling film. What can I do you for?"

The available room – there was only one – was at the top of the building, overlooking the beach. Colin followed the man down a dingy passage between the public and lounge bars, dodging the crates and boxes dumped at irregular intervals. As they approached the stairs, the man introduced himself as the landlord, Jim, and offered a damp hand speckled with breadcrumbs that had escaped the protective cling film. It gave the ensuing handshake an unpleasantly granular feel that stayed with Colin for some hours to come.

After a couple of flights and an ill-lit landing, his view of Jim's broad back and sagging cords yielded to a door. Jim produced a key, dwarfed by the size of the bear attached to it, and thrust it in the lock. A violent twist was accompanied by a heaving of the handle and the door snapped open.

"There's a knack to it," said Jim. "Lift and turn. Got that?"

"Lift and turn."

"I'll be downstairs if you need me. Luggage in the car, is it?"

It was simpler to say yes. As Jim's footsteps receded, Colin could hear the sound of opera coming from the floor below. Verdi? Puccini? He could never remember.

The room, themed in shades of aquamarine and blue, was surprisingly comfortable and surprisingly spacious. He had feared a poky attic in which he could not breathe. Two narrow dormers were set into the sloping ceiling. A faint stripe of moonlight shimmered on the surface of the sea, murmuring steadily in the darkness. He lay on the bed, kicked off his shoes and settled back with his book.

When he woke, he wondered where he was. His tea

was cold, the packet of shortbread unopened. The creaking and scraping outside the door were no doubt the sort of noises to be expected in a building of this age on a chilly night in early spring. On the other hand. A quick lift and turn and the door was open. A slab of butter-coloured light lay on the carpet outside. He looked to left and right and over the banisters to the stairs rising to meet him. Nothing. Not a sausage. Just the distant merriment of the evening's clientele and the clinking and clanking of glasses.

Chicken pie and chips swiftly demolished, he pushed into the lounge bar with the remains of his Curate's Winkle. He felt foolish holding a bear but where was he to put it? It was too big to fit in his pocket and he could hardly trouble the busy bar staff. There was no sign of Jim: how the landlord had managed to conceal the beast en route to the room was a mystery.

He found a table in a corner and placed the furry fob beside him on the red plush banquette. The walls of the lounge were covered in cream anaglypta, heavily patterned and much discoloured, but largely concealed by framed posters and photographs. The posters, as far as he could see, were all from the Darlington Theatre and featured productions of the old Sanderling Rep. *Our Town*, the final performance mentioned by the woman in the tourist office, hung a little to his right. He struggled to make out the black-and-white photographs that flanked it. He thought he recognised startlingly young versions of actors now enjoying celebrity on screens large and small. Others he did not know at all.

"A tad before your time, I fancy." A man with sandy hair, greying at the temples, pulled up a stool and deposited gin and tonic on the small round table. He was dressed entirely in beige, but for a paisley cravat in mustard, magenta and lime. "You don't mind if we join you. I'm Ray. As in sunshine!" He gave Colin's hand a manly shake and waved in the direction of the small, bird-like woman teetering towards them. "This is Florence with the supplies."

"Oh, do please call me Flo." She piled several bags of nuts next to the drinks. "I'm partial to a salted cashew," she confided, opening her first bag deftly with a rapid double-handed action. "But we don't know *your* name, young man. We haven't seen you here before."

Colin identified himself, pushing the bear behind him, and asked about the photographs.

"Rescued from the Darlington," said Flo. "They used to hang in the green room. That was our home from home at one time."

"We never missed a performance at the Rep," said Ray, slurping his gin and tonic. "We have a complete run of programmes…"

"…and rubbed shoulders with many an actor and actress after the show. That's Bunty Fisher up there. You may know her from *Wot a Whoppa!* and that Dracula thing…"

"*Fangs for the Mammary*," chimed Ray.

"*Twilight in Transylvania*, I think it was. Below her is

Everard Slope. Such a charming man. That's Audrey Fretwell to his right: a stalwart of period drama on the box on a Sunday night. And there's dear old Phyllis Richmond. She was a witch in one of the Harry Potter films…"

"Ended up on the cutting room floor," said Ray, grabbing a fistful of cashews.

"She gave me a simply marvellous recipe for spotted dick. I swear by it. Next to her we have Cosmo Blathering…"

Colin felt his attention wandering. He grunted at what he hoped were appropriate moments and thought about another pint of Curate's Winkle.

"You'll recognise Russell Whimsey, of course. He toured the length and breadth with his one-man show about humour in Shakespeare…"

"*Get Thee to a Punnery*," said Ray.

"I'm afraid it was," said Flo, chomping furiously. The smell of masticated cashews was becoming offensive. Colin tried to edge away but his freedom for manoeuvre was constrained by the bear to his rear and moving further from Flo merely put him closer to Ray.

"The two photos by the light switch…"

He twisted sharply and looked to his left.

"…are none other than Howard Desmond and Celerity Box."

He peered intently at the couple framed identically in black, both pictures signed with a flourish in faded violet ink. Howard Desmond in timeless robes, with enormous head, protruding eyes, hair like a lion's mane.

Celerity Box, self-consciously demure in all-purpose Elizabethan dress.

"I've heard of them," he said. "Are they still alive?"

"They are indeed," said Ray. "And kicking. Or at least shuffling purposefully when last we saw them. They don't get into the town so often these days. They must be well into their eighties by now."

"They're among Sanderling's most distinguished residents," said Flo. "I can't think why he was denied a knighthood. It's shameful."

"Sorry. I just thought…. They live locally, then?"

"Beyond the north sands, heading towards Dotterel. It's the big house above the beach, surrounded by trees."

So, they're still in the land of the living, thought Colin, and provide some sort of Sanderling acting connection, however tenuous. And they were present at Bryony's last known public performance, according to Ken Westow. Perhaps he should pay them a visit.

He woke early the following day. A soft peach-tinted glow had replaced the darkness of the night. Through the nearer dormer he surveyed the empty beach, shimmering orange-brown in the early morning sun. A Friday colour, he thought. In the sky, a scribble of cloud and a handful of seagulls, their raucous and insistent cries muted in deference to the hour.

He creaked downstairs after an invigorating shower. He felt almost human, despite the enforced recycling of yesterday's clothes. A visit to an all-night chemist after his escape from the beige embrace of Ray and Flo had yielded toothpaste and other essentials.

There was no sign of life on the ground floor. The all-pervasive stench of stale beer made him feel slightly sick as he scrawled a note saying he was coming back for breakfast. He slipped it under the right arm of the bear he propped against the till in the public bar.

He let himself out carefully. The air was cold and clear. He took the board walk past quiet cottages, pink and white and forget-me-not blue. Tamarisk and rosemary spilled over paling at the front. Further on, larger houses with verandas, empty chairs, looking towards the sea. The board walk stopped abruptly. He crunched on through the shingle, not the uniform brown he had seen from the window of his room but resolved, close-at-hand, into its constituent parts. Rust and ochre, cream, charcoal and grey.

A regiment of beach huts, ranged on stilts, shuttered and still. Mobile homes huddled behind newly-planted holly hedges. Shingle gave way to coarse-grained sand. There, the traces of a fire in a gentle hollow, surrounded by lumps of blackened stone. It was still warm. He crouched and picked at the charred remains. A pencil, some cloth-covered buttons, scraps of lined yellow paper, as if torn from the sort of American legal pad he used to use himself. And a mask, blistered and scorched in places but otherwise free from damage. Made of papier mâché, and dotted with sequins, it sparkled purple and gold as he turned it in the sun. It would not have looked out of place at a Venetian masked ball. Pretty incongruous lying on an English beach, though. No doubt it was left over from a fancy dress party but why try to destroy it?

A track emerged from a field in which horses were grazing. It curved away from the beach and climbed towards an area of trees by which it was absorbed. Colin followed the sharp, flinty path past banks of bramble and thick grass until he came to a high wall topped by straggling pines. Patches of render had fallen to the ground here and there to reveal the orange-red brick beneath. He was too close to the wall to see what lay behind it.

The studded door set tightly between two piers had no handle or other visible means of opening. Yet the worn stone step spoke of years of coming and going. He pushed against the door. A harsh metallic click, then nothing. The door did not move at all.

The track wound through a small copse of oak and ash, the wall a constant presence between the trees. He caught glimpses of the ridge of a roof, a weather vane in the shape of a dragon, tall chimneys, some single, some grouped. He emerged by a pair of wide wooden gates, much the same height as the wall and crowned with spikes. To one side, a block of limestone with letters incised and picked out in reddish gold: KEMBLE PLACE. As he backed away from the gates, other features came into view: the top of a tower, a half-timbered gable, part of a window, tile-hung walls: components of a big house above the beach. This, surely, was the home of Howard Desmond and Celerity Box. No sign of life, no obvious way of slipping in quietly, but at least he knew where it was now. He would have to come back.

"I thought you'd done a runner," said Jim, stretching to replace the glasses on the shelf above the bar. He stabbed his dripping brow with a handkerchief that may once have been clean and disappeared through a door to the passage. Four beeps and a chirrup and Jim was back, bearing coffee and a pile of bacon, egg and mushroom. The large oval plate had a crest in the form of a frisky young mermaid, the name of the pub stretched beneath as if to resolve any lingering doubt.

"Sorry. I was gone for longer than I meant," said Colin, installing himself at the small round table on which his breakfast had been placed.

"Not to worry. Seduced by the delights of Sanderling, I shouldn't wonder. It's easily done."

"I walked along the beach to Kemble Place. It's like Fort Knox." Jim looked blank. "Where Howard Desmond lives. At least, I assume…"

"Ah, yes, the AC-TOR. A bit of a recluse. Rarely ventures out. I still think of it as 'The Red House'. That's what it was called at one time. He changed the name. Don't ask me why."

Colin skewered a chunk of mushroom and dipped it in the egg. "Rather large for an elderly couple," he said.

"Such are the rewards of success. I expect they have live-in staff to run it. By the way, something came for you while you were out."

"But nobody knows I'm here."

Jim leaned over the bar, lifted an envelope from beside the till and passed it to him.

He turned it over slowly. It was buff and bore no name or address. "How do you know it's for me?"

"That's what the man said, apparently."

"Didn't you see him?"

"I was upstairs. My daughter took it and brought it to me before she went to school."

Colin unpeeled the envelope and shook out the contents: a photograph of him crouched on a beach, holding something in his hand, and a piece of lined yellow paper folded in half. He flicked it open, turned it round, and read the words printed in neat block capitals: '*Why, he is the prince's jester: a very dull fool…*'

He finished his breakfast, settled up and walked quickly back into town by way of narrow lanes and weedy snickets, hoping that none was a dead-end. He felt stupid and powerless. Even the gulls on the roof tops were shrieking with laughter. He had seen not a soul on the beach but someone had been there watching, waiting, biding his time. What did these people want?

Sanderling Public Library was a pale building, long and low, set back from the high street behind the war memorial. In a small garden to one side, separated from the pavement by hedges of neatly clipped box, pale pink sprays of flowering cherry nodded gently above the amethyst shades of pansies coming into bloom. Colin approached the designated inquiry point and asked to see the electoral roll.

"You mean the register of electors, do you not, young man?" said the woman behind the desk. She reminded him of Freda Axton (Miss), late Headmistress of St George's, known throughout the school as 'The Battleaxe'.

He murmured assent and shifted his weight from one foot to the other.

"Would that be the full register or the edited version?"

"Er...the full, I suppose."

"You suppose? Do you not know?"

He stood up straight. "Definitely the full."

"It is available for inspection, under supervision. You may take notes but that is all. This is not for commercial purposes, I trust."

He was left in a small windowless room lined with metal shelves, oozing magazines, journals and sundry periodicals. He kept the door open with the round stool designed to help people reach the items at the top. His supervisor was a spotty youth, one Jason Crest, according to the badge clinging to the limp pocket of his polyester shirt. Jason yawned loudly and extracted a puzzle book from the back of his trousers. Colin prepared to set to but rapidly discovered that with no idea of the address of the property there was little he could do. He coughed and asked Jason for a street atlas. The youth grunted, waved at a shelf and resumed his puzzling.

Colin concluded that Kemble Place was the isolated blob shown at the end of Sandy Lane, a narrow thoroughfare that led off the Dotterel Road. The register listed at that address not only the celebrated acting couple but several other occupants too. Charles James Fox, Frank Meadows, Aurelia Jane Potts, Charity Wise. About their age, status and function the register was silent. Maybe they were live-in staff, as Jim had suggested.

He jotted down such information as he had gleaned, announced his departure to his so-called supervisor, and headed for the local history section. He worked his way from left to right, laboriously checking the index of each volume for two names: 'Kemble Place' and 'The Red House'. He found no references to the first in any of the books. Hardly surprising, he thought, if the change of name was fairly recent. The second cropped up in *Highways and Byways in Sanderling and the Surrounding Coast*, a work by Mrs Ronald Walters first published in 1908 and reprinted without revision some twenty years later.

The book was decorated with pencil illustrations of sailing barges, boat-yards, weather-boarded houses, and winding streets, the town little more than a fishing village before it was engulfed by suburban villas. One new building in the vanguard, if somewhat larger and more isolated than the rest, was 'The Red House'. Mrs Walters was enthusiastic. 'This charming residence, built in the vernacular style for J E Turnbull Esq, has the modern convenience of electrification and enjoys a most delightful prospect atop a sandy knoll.' To Colin's eye, the accompanying sketch showed a building that was bulky and lop-sided, a mishmash of styles, details and materials. Whether the high walls he had seen were contemporary or a later addition he could not tell but they were pretty effective in obscuring the place from public view.

As he arrived at the station, passengers were trickling from the London train in ones and twos. He collided with a small girl running ahead of her mother in floods of tears.

"Bloody woman," she said. "She forgot the celery salt. I'm never going to eat quails' eggs again."

"Rosie, darling. Do come back. I'm sure Mummy can get some in Sanderling."

"Right little madam," said the man in the ticket office. "Last time it was jelly babies that caused the trouble. A girl of catholic tastes, you might say."

It was still light when Colin got back to Mafeking Avenue. He swirled his jacket onto the back of a kitchen chair and removed two items: the picture of Bryony, now tired and bent, and the notebook with his library jottings. He looked at both, sat back and sighed. He was at a loss to know what to think. The woman in the charity shop could have been wrong about seeing Bryony but she had seemed so sure that it was her. Yet if Bryony had been wandering about Sanderling with hair uncut only a couple of weeks ago how did she come to be in Oxbourne so soon afterwards, de-tressed and distressed, apparently having escaped from captivity?

He twisted and pulled the buff envelope from his jacket pocket. The photograph, like the previous one, was printed on a sheet of A4, folded crisply in half.

Someone had worked fast. The words on yellow paper rang a small bell but he could not place them. '*Why, he is the prince's jester: a very dull fool…*' He felt a very dull fool. He retrieved the other envelope from the dresser and compared the writing of the two quotations. Black ink, neat block capitals, with the hint of a flourish suppressed. The same hand, by the look of it. But whose hand he had no idea.

His thoughts turned to Howard Desmond and his wife, Celerity Box. They had not been seen on stage for years, as far as he knew, and rarely ventured from Kemble Place. It was, as Mrs Walters had observed a century earlier, 'a goodly step from the centre of the town', even using the horseless form of transport whose spread she had rightly foreseen. On the other hand, as he had shown, it was by no means impossible for younger, fitter people to make the journey by walking along the beach. Could that account for the sand Bryony had left on the floor of the donkey shop?

He fetched the laptop from his bedroom and set it up on the kitchen table. Googling 'Howard Desmond' produced a long list of entries. The most informative he found was on *mystage.com*:

> 'Howard George Merryweather Desmond was born in 1927 in Tisbury, Wiltshire. An only child, he was raised by his aunt and uncle following the death of his parents in a boating accident on Lake Garda. Sent as a boarder to St Mungo's College in a remote part of

Westmoreland (now subsumed in Cumbria), he acted regularly in school productions and turned his hand briefly to direction. Following some years in the family brewery business, and a spell of national service, he decided to pursue an acting career, enrolling in 1951 at the David Garrick Academy of Dramatic Art. Here he met his future wife and life-long acting partner, Celerity Box, whom he married in 1953. They formed one of the most famous and enduring marriages in show business.

'Desmond made his stage debut at the Theatre Royal, Northampton, working seasons in weekly rep first there and later in Buxton, Hull and Leatherhead. In 1963, he took over the running of the company at Hornchurch, starring (with his wife) in the play that made their name: *Glad Tidings*. The production transferred to the West End, where, over the following years, the couple appeared in a string of light comedy successes. Chief amongst these were: *Summon up the Blood*, *Darker than Moss*, *The Olive Grove* and *Oodles of Noodles*. As director at Sanderling in the 1970s, Desmond returned to the classical repertoire, with celebrated interpretations of Chekov and Shakespeare. His *Uncle Vanya* and *King Lear* were particular personal triumphs.

'With the demise of the Sanderling Rep in 1986, the focus of Desmond's career switched to character parts in film and television, media he had hitherto espoused only occasionally. His guest appearance as The Dark One in *Dr Who* earned him a cult following for a while. After several fallow years, he secured the part of Stan the barman in the short-lived series *Make Mine a Stiff One*, in which his wife appeared as the irrepressible Marge.

'Howard Desmond and Celerity Box were both appointed CBE in 1987 for services to the theatre.'

No reference to his Abanazer at Hornchurch, thought Colin. Perhaps not a jewel in the acting crown. Still, it looked as though the Desmonds had been out of work, or retired, for years. What on earth had they been doing all this time? Enjoying a leisurely and uneventful existence in a large house atop a sandy knoll? Possibly, but somehow he doubted it.

Eight

'O *brave monster! Lead the way.*' The heavy green curtains
swished efficiently to a close as Caliban staggered off,
bottle in hand, Stephano and Trinculo bringing up the
rear. The applause was vigorous and prolonged. The
gently swaying lanterns that passed for house lights
brightened by fits and starts, dispersing the shadows,
exposing heads, mostly grey, that bobbed and twisted
and rose as thoughts turned to interval drinks in the
makeshift bar in the foyer.

Colin had only just made it, stumbling over feet and
handbags in semi-darkness to find his seat. The church
hall doors that he had pummelled and shaken on his
previous visit had admitted him without demur thirty
seconds before the performance was due to begin.

Progress to the bar was slow as the last-night audience
pottered and prattled, shuffled and blethered its way to
an area set up with trestle tables offering a choice of
wine, beer, fruit juice and coffee. Hemmed in and held

back, he felt the panic rising within him. He forced his way to the front. A hasty exchange of coin and lager and he was out, breathing heavily in the mild spring garden in front of the hall.

He sat on a bench and decanted the amber liquid slowly into the glass he had been given without having to ask. Asking for a glass had been a recurring embarrassment for him, and source of amusement for everyone else, while he had been away. How English! they said. How charming, how quaint.

His decision to turn up to the play had been a last-minute one. Looking back in weeks to come on the events of that night, he was unable to rationalise the series of impulsive actions other than in terms of some vague sense that Bryony was here somewhere and that he needed to be at the scene of her final public performance. He had left an overnight bag at the Mermaid in the safe-keeping of Jim's wife, who promised to have it taken to his room while he hastened, bear-free, to the hall in Victoria Road.

It was nearly time for the second half. Give it a bit longer, he thought. Better a few stubbed toes in row P than facing the crowd in the foyer. He drained his glass and was about to go back when a car screeched to a halt at the gate. The driver slid out, opened the rear door and offered an arm in support of two figures easing onto the pavement. As they approached the path to the hall, Colin shrank back into the shadows. He could not make out their facial features in any detail but there was no mistaking the large head and leonine profile of Howard Desmond. His pale companion was surely Celerity Box.

Colin followed at a discreet distance. From the rear, the couple seemed pretty robust, not at all the frail and faltering pair he had imagined. Their progress was briefly interrupted by the fawn and fawning intrusion of Ray and Flo, too focused on renewing old acquaintance to notice him across the hall. They were perhaps the only other members of the audience who recognised the duo now making for their seats at the front. Picking his way to his own seat, he did not see the man with the maroon tie standing at the back, jiggling car keys in his pocket as he tilted a bottle of beer.

'As you from crimes would pardon'd be, / Let your indulgence set me free.' Ken Westow, standing in for the Enigma's advertised Prospero, Oswald Farleigh, led the cast forward as the audience showed warm appreciation in the traditional manner. No piercing whoops or whistles in Sanderling, thank you very much. A hasty insertion in the programme claimed that Oswald was indisposed. "Indisposed as a newt," said a woman in the row behind. "I saw him in the Sailor's after the matinée. He could hardly stand." Either way, thought Colin, Ken's performance was remarkably confident and assured: perhaps Oswald Farleigh was often indisposed.

He loitered in the garden as the audience dispersed. The foyer, it seemed, was being re-arranged for the after-show party. A van drew up and disgorged black-shirted youths bearing trays of food and additional supplies of beer and wine. Through a gap between door and doorframe, he could see members of the cast arriving in dribs and drabs from the general direction of the dressing rooms behind the stage and making for the bar. A small group had formed a semi-circle around Howard Desmond and Celerity Box, a finely featured woman with hair the colour of pale straw. Some sort of discussion was being mediated by Ken, newly restored to denim suit and apricot shirt.

The couple were obviously staying for the party. How long did he have? His first thought was to try and hide in the boot of their car. The absurdity of the idea did not take long to strike him. There was a taxi office at the station but he remembered a small rank in the high street near the leisure centre. He stole out of the garden and into Victoria Road, heading for Albert Terrace and the centre of town.

He asked the taxi driver to drop him in the Dotterel Road, at the turn-off to Sandy Lane.

"There's nothing here, mate. Just the big house at the end."

"This is fine, thanks."

In truth, it was far from fine. Sandy Lane was unlit and the moon, hidden by low cloud, could offer no relief. The road was little more than a rough track winding tightly through dense dark pine. He groped forward, tripped by unseen stones and snatched without warning by brambles trailing from the wood. Behind, a faint orange glow marked Sanderling and its environs; ahead, there was nothing. He was beginning to wish he had let the taxi take him all the way to Kemble Place but it had not looked so far on the map in the library and he had not wanted the noise of a car to alert whoever remained in the house.

Suddenly, a security light snapped on, temporarily blinding him and bathing the road a brilliant silvery-white. As his eyes adjusted, he saw the familiar high brick wall but not the house on the other side. He stepped to the wall and the light went off, enveloping him again in thick darkness. This time, he had the wall as a guide. He followed it to the double gates at the end and curved round the corner into the gathering of trees beyond. He steadied himself against the trunk of an ash and sank down to wait.

The quiet of the night was broken by a low grumbling. Two shafts of light pierced the black as a car rounded the last bend. Moments later, the security light threw the vehicle into sharp relief. It was an old but shiny Daimler. The Desmonds were back.

The car drew up in front of the gates. Two beeps and they opened slowly inwards with a contented hum. As the car proceeded towards the house the gates began to close. The security light snapped off just as another illuminated the outsize half-timbered porch to which the couple were being delivered. Colin took his chance. He slipped through the narrowing gap and ducked out of sight. Now what?

The front door banged, the Daimler sauntered round the side. It was dark again. He pushed through foliage of differing degrees of resistance, jostled and stroked and scratched as he progressed. This was not doing his jacket any good at all, he reflected. The drive would have been a good deal simpler but he had to avoid the scrunching of gravel and the risk of setting off another light. He emerged by some sort of low wooden structure from which a path appeared to lead. He followed it and crashed painfully into a wheel barrow, spilling tools onto the path.

A powerful beam stabbed the darkness, revealing spade, fork, shovel and rake clustered in a random heap. "Good evening, Mr Mallory. At Kemble Place we tend to do our gardening during the daylight hours. We find it's easier to see. May I suggest that you come with me."

Colin was stunned into silence. How on earth did this man know he was there? How did he know his name? There was nowhere to run, nowhere to hide. He allowed himself to be led to the old stable block. The room they entered had been converted into an office. Another man was sitting at a desk at one end, watching a television screen as he sipped a gigantic mug of tea.

"Well, well, well," he said. "Christmas has come early this year, has it not, Charles?"

"It has indeed, Frank."

"We enjoyed your performance, Mr Mallory." He waved at the screen. The picture changed every so often to show various camera positions inside and outside the grounds. "Most enterprising. Shows great promise, does it not, Charles?"

"Great promise, Frank. I do believe that Mr Mallory was inspired by his visit to the church hall."

"It stimulated him."

"Fired him up."

"Just the sort of person we need, is he not, Charles?"

"Eminently suitable, I'd say, Frank."

"But he will need to speak."

"He will. It must be stage fright."

"A temporary loss of transmission."

"If you'll open the gate, I'll walk back to Sanderling," said Colin.

"He's broken his silence, Frank."

"He has a sense of humour, Charles."

"Just let me go. I've obviously made a mistake."

"A cool customer, Frank."

"Very cool, Charles. But it's not the plan."

"Not the plan at all."

"He hasn't read the script."

"We're disappointed, Mr Mallory."

"Very disappointed."

"Considering the trouble."

"A lot of trouble."

"Is this some sort of joke?"

"Sir doesn't make jokes, does he, Frank?"

"Indeed, not, Charles."

"But perhaps it's time."

"I rather think it is."

"May I suggest, Mr Mallory, that you tidy yourself in the adjacent bathroom before we adjourn to the house."

Charles led him out of the stable block across a cobbled yard that glistened in the restrained light of a new moon making a belated appearance through the thinning grey cloud. He took a key to a heavy panelled door and proceeded down a bare passageway relieved by elaborate terrazzo flooring. At the end, hooks hung with coats, boots standing to attention underneath, a pair of fire extinguishers lending colour to the scene. Through another door, top half glazed, and along a carpeted corridor with prints and maps grouped on pale cream walls.

"Not much further, Mr Mallory."

Up a few steps and into a small but comfortable room with a large portrait in oils above the fireplace. It was a man wearing a tweed suit, a gold watch chain and a benevolent smile.

"Is Sir ready for us?" This to a homely woman, who rose quickly from an armchair, put down her magazine and smoothed her ample skirt.

"He wants you to have a word with him first."

"Mrs Potts will hold the fort," said Charles, giving a slight bow. It was only now Colin registered that the charcoal suit, crisp white shirt and maroon tie were the uniform of a chauffeur.

"You can call me Aurelia, like the others. I'm looking forward to getting to know you. You're looking tired, dear. Would you like a cup of tea?"

*

Their footsteps on the cold tiled floor clacked around the hall. Colin caught snatches of dark panelling, paintings, wooden stairs, a large vase of dried flowers. It was well after midnight. Everything was becoming a blur. He just wanted to sleep. Charles stopped outside a door, knocked, and turned the gleaming brass handle. "Mr Mallory for you, Sir."

"Ah, Colin. Come in, come in. We've been expecting you. Sit down, dear boy. I do hope the team have been looking after you."

Howard Desmond sat upright in a winged chair, hands clasped over the top of a cane. A gold signet ring shone in the light of a standard lamp.

"What am I doing here? I need to get back to Sanderling."

"A curious question, if I may say so. You made your way from the town and entered the grounds of your own accord, did you not? Some might say, 'broke in'. Would you rather we summoned the local constabulary?"

"I have a room at the Mermaid. They'll be wondering where I am."

"Oh, I don't think so. We took the precaution of picking up your things on the way here. Charles told them that you wouldn't be needing the room after all."

"Said he'd made alternative arrangements, Sir."

"Exactly. So you see, Colin, there's no pressing need to get back, no need at all. We may have to kit you out a little more extensively in due course but there's no rush, is there Charles?"

"All taken care of, Sir."

"I'll be leaving in the morning."

"That's a trifle sooner than we had in mind. And no way to repay our hospitality. Were you thinking of scaling the walls or perhaps breaking down the gates?"

"Escaping like a prisoner, you mean. Is that what I am?"

"Strong words, Colin. I prefer to think of you as our guest. We provide bed and board in return for your services."

"What services? What are you talking about?"

"All in good time. All in good time. The hour is late. I suggest we resume our discussion in the morning. Is Colin's room prepared, Charles?"

"It is indeed, Sir."

"Then I bid you good night." Howard Desmond stood up slowly and turned to leave.

"Is this what you did to Bryony?" said Colin. He wanted to shout but it came out as a whimper.

"Ah, were you looking for someone?"

"You know I was. Is she locked up here too?"

"I think you need some rest and one of Aurelia's cooked breakfasts. Charles will show you to your room."

Nine

*H*e could not think where he was when he opened his eyes. A haze of unfamiliar shapes and colours in the half-light. Then it all came back with a jolt. He turned slowly on the hard mattress and propped himself on an elbow. He ached all over and the backs of his hands were scratched. He reached for the glass on the bedside cabinet and sipped tentatively. The water tasted dusty and faintly metallic. He took in panelling, pale and strangely grained with wave-like patterns and contours. The walls above were green, yellowy-green, more willow than apple, he thought, as he pushed the pillows against the headboard and sat back.

Instinctively, he turned to look at his watch, then remembered that he had handed it over to Charles the night before, along with his mobile phone.

"You won't be needing these here, Mr Mallory. We'll look after them for you, keep them safe."

He was appalled at the recollection of his own

passivity, meekly following Charles up stairs and along passageways without further protest or attempt at escape. He had been in a daze, tired and trapped, with neither the strength nor the will to do anything other than sleep. And how did they know he had a room at the Mermaid? He had only rung the pub after he had scrambled on to the train to Sanderling, ignoring whistles and shouts to stand away.

He lowered himself to the floor and on to a rug, a soft and comforting confusion of burnt orange, grey and the darkest blue. He was supported by the bed, a wash stand and the back of a chair in his halting progress towards the window. He fumbled and pulled the cord he found at one end of the curtains. They swished smoothly to reveal a broad band of nacreous sky and narrower strips of sea and beach beneath, a view uninhibited, at this height, by the pines and other vegetation in the grounds. If he had been in the mood he might well have agreed with Mrs Ronald Walters that the house afforded 'a most delightful prospect'.

He wondered what time it was. As if on cue, a bell sounded tinnily from somewhere inland. The quarter hour? Half hour? Either way, it took him no further forward. How long was he going to be left here? Or was he expected to find his own way to wherever Aurelia's cooked breakfasts were to be had, always assuming he was not too late? He had eaten nothing since the baguette, crammed with sweating salami and the occasional gherkin, snatched in haste at a station buffet before he caught his connection to Sanderling. It was only yesterday but it seemed a world away.

As he turned to face the room, he saw that his clothes, such as they were, had been laid out carefully on a large chest, shoes paired neatly at the base. When had that happened? He saw also that the room had two doors. He must have entered through one of them but he was hard put to say which. He hobbled to the door to his left and turned the handle. It was a bathroom, not contemporary with the house but installed fairly recently, by the look of it. His washing things were in their places by the basin.

Showered and dressed, he felt a little less stiff, a little more awake. He moved towards the other door. He was suddenly grabbed by panic. Surely he would not have been locked in all night? What if there had been a fire? He lunged. The door opened with ease. He closed it quietly behind him and stole onto the landing. It was unexpectedly bright, illuminated by an enormous skylight resembling a miniature greenhouse or conservatory. He must be at the top of the house. He looked over the balustrade at the broad stairs falling away below but could not see how to reach them.

The landing led to an archway of the pointed gothic variety. A red velvet curtain was drawn across it. As he approached, he saw, ranged to his right, a row of mahogany cabinets, roughly waist-high, pushed against the wall. Each had a series of drawers, increasing in depth from top to bottom. He paused and knelt awkwardly in front of the nearest cabinet, taking a pair of neatly turned wooden handles between thumb and forefinger. The top drawer slid towards him, revealing butterflies pinned to cream-coloured board or cork beneath a sheet of glass. Under each one was a label with English and Latin names in sharp black copperplate. He opened other drawers, other cabinets, every one filled with lepidoptera as fresh and bright as the day they were caught. A few – red admiral, peacock, large white – he recognised as visitors to the buddleia at Mafeking Avenue. Most were quite unknown to him.

He found the experience curiously depressing. So much time, so much trouble to trap and kill so many. Still, at least they were preserved for posterity, if posterity could be found on the uppermost floor of an Edwardian house 'atop a sandy knoll'. Perhaps they were here when Howard Desmond and his lovely etc moved in. He could hardly see either of them roaming the countryside with butterfly net and killing bottle at the ready.

He rose to his feet, steadying himself momentarily on the corner of a cabinet. He was struck by the unrelenting silence. No voices, no footsteps, no banging doors, not even a ticking clock. Nothing. Where was everyone?

He slid the rings of the velvet curtain along the slim brass pole above it and ducked through the archway. He found himself in a shadowy corridor that terminated abruptly at a door marked PRIVATE. It was locked. There was only one way to go.

He followed the crooked course of a narrow staircase

off to the right, guided in the semi-dark by a bulbous banister, smooth, almost fluid, in the palm of his hand. The staircase came out at the top of the main stairs that he had seen from the floor above. The area was bathed in brilliance from the massive skylight. It took a few moments for his eyes to adjust. He sloped past portraits of people he did not know, some severe, some benign, some verging on the flighty, others just plain bored. He was starving. Thoughts of a cooked breakfast brought back memories of the blueberry pancakes, crispy bacon and maple syrup that were his staple at the Harvard diner off Massachusetts Avenue, until a thickening waistline drove him to the yoghurt with granola and fresh fruit.

He landed in the hall, the space somehow clearer and better defined than it had been last night. Still not a sound, not a sign of life. He gave the front door a twist and a tug, if only for form's sake, but it was as unyielding as he had expected. He met the beady eye of a large stuffed cockatoo, staring glassily from a case on the hall table, its sulphurous crest a perfect match for the daffodils placed nearby.

He tried the door to the book-lined room where he had met Howard Desmond. It opened no more readily than others leading off the hall. There was just one left. He grabbed the handle, turned and fell into pitch darkness. He came to rest on something soft. Suddenly, the room was a blaze of light. Curtains were drawn back, ceremonial music blasted from a corner, followed by vigorous applause from figures in maroon tracksuits ranged on either side of the Chinese carpet. At the far end, two people sitting on identical gilt chairs: Howard Desmond and Celerity Box, smiling indulgently as Colin found his feet.

Desmond raised a hand and the clapping ceased.

"Good morning, good morning. I bid you welcome to Kemble Place. I trust that you slept well, my boy. We have been awaiting your arrival with eager anticipation. We followed your progress since you left your room, you see, and timed our assembly accordingly." He waved towards one of the cameras that, as Colin now realised, were placed at strategic points throughout the house. "Foolishly, we failed to foresee your keen interest in butterflies and moths. I'm sure we can find a suitable guide or handbook in the library that will help to enrich your stay." More indulgent smiles and laughter from the company.

"Insolent retinue!"

The noise stopped immediately. Was the man serious or not? It was hard to tell. In the light of day he looked much older, thought Colin, his body dominated by the enormous head and mass of curled grey hair, his skin deeply scored like the bark of an ancient oak. Celerity Box, by his side, seemed slight in comparison, as delicate and as fragile as a china doll.

"Do sit down. It's time to introduce you to your new friends and colleagues. You'll be working closely together."

"I could do with something to eat. Then I'm going."

"Oh dear. I think you may have the wrong idea,

young Colin. We've gone to a lot of trouble to bring you to Kemble Place. A lot of time and effort."

"And expense," put in Celerity Box.

"You can't keep me here. People know where I am. They'll come looking."

"I hardly think so."

"I'll be missed."

"By your vast number of acquaintances? Surely not. We've squared the estimable Mrs Nolan, who will no doubt liaise with your elder sibling in due course."

"You're not treating me like you have Bryony. Where is she anyway?"

"A spirited defence, but becoming a trifle tedious. Not to say lacking in gratitude. And what treatment, pray, are we supposed to have meted out to your friend Bryony?"

"You know perfectly well. Pursued her, held her captive, cut off her hair."

"Now why should we have done that? I do believe there's been a misunderstanding. Bryony is no more here against her will than the rest of the crew." He took them in with a sweep of his arm. They were annoyingly good-natured and relaxed. "Do they look like prisoners? People are free to come and go, after a certain period of probation. Think of us as a family you're about to join."

"I'm not joining anything."

"Bryony *will* be disappointed."

"*Bryony?*"

"But of course. She suggested you in the first place.

How else would we have known of your talents? Let us adjourn to breakfast, people."

Colin tried to work out, take in the implications of this news as he found himself enveloped in maroon and guided to the panelled dining room next door. He was installed at a large refectory table. Aurelia greeted him cheerily and set before him a plate piled with scrambled egg, bacon, sausage, black pudding and mushroom. Coffee and orange juice followed swiftly. Howard Desmond and Celerity Box took up position at either end of the table, with others filling in the spaces in between. On the opposite side of the room, he noticed a smaller table to which Aurelia herself repaired when everyone else had been served. She joined Frank and Charles and a middle-aged woman whose face was vaguely familiar, though he was sure he had never seen her before. Perhaps this was Charity, the one name on the electoral roll as yet unaccounted for.

"Hi," came a voice from his left. "I'm Ted Gowanus from Brooklyn, New York. Glad to meet you." He had short black hair and a pudgy face. He thrust out a hand for Colin to shake. It was soft and moist and faintly clinging. "I've only been here a few months myself. Ever since Sir took me under his wing." He looked much the same age as Colin and had no doubt been deputed to take the lead in making the introductions. With the Desmonds only feet away, there was no chance of asking the sort of questions Colin really wanted answered. Why was everyone so placid, anyway, so accepting of the situation in which they found themselves? Hypnosis, perhaps, or some sort of drug-induced euphoria? Or maybe they were actually here voluntarily. In any case, he thought, there seemed little option but to play along with whatever it was that went on at Kemble Place, to gain their trust, biding time and an opportunity to make his escape.

Ted went round the table, prompting beams and greetings from the half dozen or so other members of the group. A pretty mixed bag, as his father would have put it. And was Brenda, the plain girl in the middle, the 'mousy little thing' the woman in the charity shop had seen with Bryony?

"Jack won the sweepstake," said Ted, pointing to his left.

"What sweepstake?"

Jack Naseby, a silver-haired man with purple-red face and bulbous nose, lowered his fork and spoke. The voice was firm and fruity.

"We placed bets on how long it would take you to find us. There was a fair amount in the kitty by the end. All in tokens, of course; there's no cash in circulation here. When Sir announced your arrival the names went in the hat."

"A panama I once wore in a little play of ours in the West End," said Howard Desmond.

"*The Olive Grove*" said Celerity Box, breathily. "Wonderful cast. Wonderful notices."

"Except from the man Hobson."

"Pure spite. He never forgave you for that incident with the melon at the Caprice. Or was it the Ivy?"

*

"We call ourselves the Kemble Players." Desmond relaxed into the embrace of the winged chair from which he had interviewed Colin briefly some hours earlier. Colin himself sat rigid on the green leather chesterfield opposite.

"After the house, I take it."

"No, no. Or only indirectly. They are both named after the actor. I refer to *John Philip* Kemble, not to his brothers Charles or Stephen." He gestured towards a series of engravings showing the actor as Richard III, Hamlet, Coriolanus and Macbeth frozen in dramatic pose on the stage of Drury Lane. "A talented family. They were all in the business, including the sisters, though rather overshadowed by the eldest, Sarah Siddons. You've heard of *her*, I trust?"

"Bryony had a postcard on her mantelpiece. A picture by Gainsborough, I think. Always reminded me of Little Bo Beep."

"For me, she is the Tragic Muse, as portrayed by Joshua Reynolds. She was painted by all the leading artists of her time, yet none, it is said, really succeeded in capturing her likeness. I suppose we shall never know for sure. Her husband, William Siddons, was himself an actor, a fellow performer in the company run by her parents." Howard Desmond paused and dabbed a watering eye with a cream silk handkerchief, slid from the top pocket of the quilted jacket he had donned since breakfast. "Mrs Siddons acted with Kemble. Some of the great roles. I like to think of my wife and I as performing in that tradition, creating opportunities here at Kemble Place denied to us by the modern commercial theatre."

"Er…"

"You think age against us? Do not underestimate the rejuvenating power of the stage. Have you not heard the expression 'Dr Theatre'?"

Colin mumbled and shook his head.

"We have assembled by various means a small company of diverse talents. Some members a good deal more experienced than others, but no matter. Versatility is our watchword. We offer training, grounding, the chance to play a range of parts. Much like the old weekly rep, albeit on a smaller scale. Cast against type: that's the key. Stretch and develop and you can turn your hand to anything. You never know what you can do until you try, young Colin."

"Why bring me here if you already have such a talented troupe?"

"Overall progress has been encouraging but, despite our best endeavours, one or two of our number have proved…unreliable. Some reassignment of roles has been called for. I wanted to expand the company in any case, inject some fresh blood. Your friend Bryony mentioned you. I have reason to trust her judgement."

"I can't think why she suggested me. I haven't acted in years, and that was only at school. She hasn't seen me since we left. You still haven't told me where she is."

"Time enough. Time enough."

"I at least need to know she's all right."

"I'm touched by your concern. As, no doubt, is she. But she joined our little band entirely voluntarily, in common with most of the others. Some have required a modicum of encouragement but the majority see advantage in dropping out of circulation for a while, in avoiding public gaze. We guarantee discretion and a safe haven for those on board."

"Since when did actors want to avoid publicity?"

"You'd be surprised, if the alternative is unwelcome attention from the authorities or persistent individuals. Here they can practise their craft, hone their skills, in privacy while providing a resident company for my wife and me. The benefit is mutual. An admirable arrangement, don't you think?"

"Surely, none of that applies to Bryony? What does she have to hide?"

"I daresay she'll explain things in due course. Tomorrow we start rehearsals for *Twelfth Night*. You shall play Feste. A *clown*. Then we shall see how you fit our plans for the longer term."

A sharp tap on the door. One, twice, three times. Bryony? Colin rolled off the bed and grabbed the handle. It was Charles with a bundle.

"Your tracksuit, Mr Mallory. Sir would be obliged if you would wear it in the house and grounds. It should be your size."

"What for? I mean, why on earth does everyone have to wear a tracksuit? It's like school uniform."

"Just members of the company, Mr Mallory, not the resident staff. Sir sees it as a means of promoting corporate spirit, a sense of identity. It shows that you're one of the team."

"But why maroon? It's a revolting colour."

"Sir considers it to be a distinguished and distinctive burgundy. This is the best we could get. Apparently chosen in honour of the Duke of Burgundy, a part cropping up in several of Shakespeare's plays and recalled by Sir with particular affection."

"He's off his trolley."

"Ours not to reason why, Mr Mallory. I'll see you in the hall in five minutes. Sir would like me to show you the theatre."

Colin followed Charles through double doors at the back of the hall and across an ill-lit lobby to a second set. He felt light-headed, outside himself, as if none of this was really happening to him. They loitered for a moment while Charles extracted a key from an inside pocket. A loud click, a firm push, and they were in. An explosion of light revealed a cube, not large, not small, forming a room that projected from the rear of the house. At the far end, the stage, a rectangular proscenium flanked by pairs of fluted pilasters topped with ionic capitals. Similar features were repeated round the walls, alternating with high windows of grey-green glass.

"It was built for Mrs Jocelyn Turnbull, wife of the first owner of the Red House, as Kemble Place was called in those days. She had a penchant for recitals and other entertainments, many laid on for charity. The servants were permitted to watch from up there."

Colin turned towards the diminutive gallery centred in the wall behind him. It could scarcely have accommodated more than two or three people at a time. "It's a bit odd," he said, resuming his course a few steps behind Charles. "The floor is flat. There's no rake and no seating, apart from a few chairs at the front."

"The theatre did duty as a ballroom in its day and served as a hospital ward in two world wars. A flexible space with a varied history, you might say. We have more chairs stacked in the corridor."

"For the audience? Who comes to see these plays?"

"Not the public, Mr Mallory. Not people from outside. That wouldn't do at all. When it comes to performances, Sir aims to create a suitably appreciative atmosphere without the inconvenience and fuss of external intrusion."

Colin selected a chocolate biscuit from the plate thrust towards him with mock servility by Ted Gowanus and took his tea to the refectory table. Vincent Kemp, down to play the Duke Orsino, slid silently along the bench to let him in.

"Are you related to the alpinist?" asked Cornelia Thrupp. Her sharp nose and intense stare reminded him of a bird of prey, possibly a bald eagle like the one his parents had seen in the Black Hills of Dakota. Surely they would be home soon and concerned at his absence.

And it was hard to believe that Clare would be fobbed off with whatever nonsense Mrs Nolan had been 'squared' to say.

"Sorry?"

"The mountaineer, George Mallory. The one that went missing on Mount Everest."

"Not as far as I know."

"Or Sir Thomas?" squeaked Brenda, the mousy girl sitting next to her. "The *Morte d'Arthur* man."

"Different spelling of 'Mallory', my little chickadee," said Cornelia, tweaking her ear with some force. "This little scrap has been chosen to play Maria, Olivia's maid. Haven't you, my lambkin?" She gave Brenda's ear another tweak and pushed her away. "And I am to play Fabian: can you imagine? A shortage of female parts, said Sir. He told me I should be grateful, that some productions drop the role entirely. Regard it as a challenge, he said. 'Stretch and develop; stretch and develop.' I should coco. Madam, of course, is cast as Olivia to you know who's Sir Toby Belch. She's supposed to be his niece, for God's sake."

"Perhaps some subtle lighting will help," said Colin.

"That falls to our friend Ted. Half geek, half nerd. He probably sleeps with a length of cable and a pair of pliers."

"How on earth did someone from Brooklyn end up here?"

"Who knows? Sometimes it's better not to ask." She glanced quickly at Vincent and then away again. "Anyway, I hear you're going to play Feste. I shall enjoy watching you fool around in your motley. Can you sing? *With hey, ho* and all that."

"I'm a bit rusty." And I'm not planning to be around long enough for anyone to hear me, he said to himself. He took a gulp of lukewarm tea. "Who's playing Viola, by the way?"

"The golden girl. Who else?" said Cornelia. "No one has a right to be that pretty. Sorry, I gather Bryony is a friend of yours."

"I knew her once, years ago. We were at school together."

"Then a happy reunion is in prospect. We must away, mustn't we my little rabbit?" She pulled roughly at Brenda's collar. "We have other duties to perform. We all have roles apart from acting, inside the grounds or out. No doubt Sir will tell you what's expected when you've settled in. Your Bryony developed a keen interest in photography."

Ten

"Ah, Feste. Just the chap. I'm doing the rounds before tomorrow."

Colin turned at the foot of the stairs as Charity Wise lumbered into the hall holding a cardboard box. She was pink in the face and out of breath.

"It's a job tracking everyone down in a place this size," she said, dropping the box to the floor. She bent down with a huff and extracted two items. "Here's a copy of the play. We decided in the end to go for the Penguin edition. Celerity B liked the cover. And this is the rehearsal schedule." She handed him a sheet of pink paper, with 'Feste' written neatly in the top right-hand corner. "It's quite simple: day 1, 2, 3 etc, time (am or pm), place, scenes involved and cast required. We start tomorrow morning with a read-through with the whole company. We don't have auditions: Sir assigns the roles and people must make the best of them. It was touch and go casting this one."

"Very good," said Colin. "Only one slight problem. I had to hand over my watch and mobile phone so how will I be able to work out the day and time?"

"It's perfectly straightforward. The rest of the cast are in the same boat. If it's am it's after breakfast; pm is after lunch. The designated number of the rehearsal day will be shown clearly on the board in the dining room alongside another copy of the schedule. The system works smoothly enough."

"Fine, but why create the problem in the first place?"

"Sir thinks that players will be better focussed if they are not distracted by things like the passage of time and people and events in the outside world. He expects, demands, total commitment."

"And gets it?"

"Of course. Or they wouldn't survive, would they?"

"I was told we were free to come and go, after some sort of probation. So there must be some contact with the world beyond Kemble Place." He thought of Bryony's trips to the charity shop with the mousy girl in tow.

"On a very limited basis and only for those who've earned Sir's trust. It is not a privilege granted lightly."

"Or abused?"

"No. Not any more. It happened just the once, not that I should be telling you. The person concerned is…no longer with us." Charity stooped to pick up her box. "I must get on. I've lost Malvolio and Sir Andrew."

He watched her shuffle back down the corridor from which she had come until she was lost to view. Something about the way she moved reinforced the vague sense of familiarity he had felt when he saw her in the dining room at breakfast. Yet he was still sure that he had not seen her before.

"A penny for them," said Tim and Tom in unison, skipping past en route to the garden door, Tim on the black squares, Tom on the white. Colin tried hard to imagine the gawky pair as Sebastian and Antonio, the one Viola's brother, the other a sea captain. He was unequal to the task. Ideal brokers men in provincial panto, perhaps, but unlikely to be found on the Illyrian shore. Maybe Howard Desmond had a sense of humour after all.

He sat on a hall chair, avoiding the glassy stare of the cockatoo on the table opposite, and looked again at the rehearsal schedule. The strawberry pink of the paper against the maroon of his tracksuit made him feel faintly queasy. The schedule was as demanding as it was detailed, with no let-up before the final technical and dress rehearsals and the performances themselves. But who would come and see them? Surely, the cast would not deliver lines to an empty auditorium. Intriguing but academic from his point of view, or so he hoped. Just as long as he could maintain a façade of acquiescence until the time came.

The sky through the fanlight above the front door was a soft, inviting rectangle of duck-egg blue. He folded the paper in four, slipped it inside his copy of the script and made for the garden door at the back of the hall. Clear of the theatre projecting from the rear of the house, he took a damp brick path past beds just beginning to come to life in the mild spring air. No sign of Tim and Tom. He headed towards a wooded area ablaze with the yellow and cream of daffodils and narcissi swathed beneath the leafless trees. The effect was dazzling.

A gap in the thick yew hedge beyond brought him to more open parts leading to the conifers that he had seen from the track on the other side. Raised beds constructed of timbers like railway sleepers no doubt yielded vegetables at the right time of year. The high wall surrounding the property was clearly visible now, topped by strands of razor wire designed, he assumed, as much to inhibit escape as to discourage unwelcome visitors. He had not, so far, spotted any obvious weakness in the defences.

A little way along, a glasshouse in a state of partial collapse clung to the wall. Terracotta flower pots of uniform shape but varying size teetered in towers at one end. A blackbird flew off with a cry of alarm as he approached the door. It was slightly ajar and opened further without much resistance. Flakes of grey-white paint spiralled to the ground as he brushed past. He made his way between disused grow bags on one side and compost-strewn staging on the other, empty seed trays piled at intervals, bunches of raffia nestling in a worm-infested trug. As he reached the point at which the roof was beginning to sag he heard the door snap to a close behind him. He spun round in fright. A figure stood by the door, motionless, head bent forward and covered by a denim cap.

"Who is it?" he croaked. His throat was dry and he could not swallow.

The figure raised its head slowly and pulled off the cap. Long golden hair tumbled about the shoulders.

"Hallo, Col. It's me."

"Bryony!" He made no move toward her. He seemed to have lost the power of speech. There were so many things to say, so many questions to ask. Where to begin?

"Aren't you pleased to see me?"

"Yes, but…"

"But what? Haven't you been looking for me?"

"Where have you been?"

"Sir thought it best if I kept out of the way for a while."

"Your hair, your face. There's nothing wrong with them."

"Thank you kindly, Mr Mallory," she said, dropping to a quick curtsey. "Some people are a bit more positive."

"You know what I mean. Your hair was hacked about and you looked ghastly. In the sketch. The one done in Oxbourne."

"I haven't been to Oxbourne in years. Not since my parents died. Why don't we go back to the house and have some tea?"

"A touching reunion, Frank. They make a handsome couple."

"They do indeed, Charles." They were in a room in the stable block, monitoring the return of Colin and Bryony to the house on a flickering television screen.

"But somewhat lacking in warmth, don't you think? Not even a chaste kiss."

"It's early days."

"Not to be rushed."

"No hurry at all."

"There are bounds, nevertheless, are there not?"

"It wouldn't do to overstep the mark."

"Sir would not be pleased."

"He'd be most unhappy."

"We shall have to keep an eye on them."

"Watch them carefully."

"Especially Mr Mallory."

"He seems a trifle wary."

"Cautious."

"On his guard."

"I do hope he's going to settle."

"Enter into the spirit."

"Not do anything foolish."

"Otherwise steps will have to be taken."

"That would be a pity."

"It would spoil the plan."

"We don't want history to repeat itself, do we Frank?"

"Indeed we do not, Charles."

Aurelia placed the tray on the low table between them and poured the tea while Colin helped himself to a spiced biscuit.

"Sir thought you might want to catch up," she said. "I'll see you're not disturbed."

"It was a test," said Bryony when Aurelia had left the room. "To see if I could deliver the goods."

"The goods being me?"

Her eyes, an even deeper blue than he remembered, flecked with gold that seemed to sparkle in the light of the standard lamp.

"We needed to find a replacement for someone who left us sooner than expected. I thought of you."

"But I haven't been back in the country five minutes."

She looked radiant but her manner was cool, business-like, unabashed.

"I know. We established where you were and things took off from there."

"So the whole thing was an elaborate hoax to lure me here. No one was after you at all." He should have listened to Clare, he reflected, focussed on getting a job, anything.

"No."

"I suppose it never occurred to you to *ask* me to join the group, in something like a conventional manner?"

"You'd never have agreed, would you? That just risked exposing the set-up here without any benefit. And, as I said, Sir saw it as a test. It was one I needed to pass."

They sipped their tea in silence for a while, avoiding each other's eyes.

Then Colin said, "You realise I was worried about you, about what might have happened to you."

"Yes. Sorry."

"And the sketch?"

"Done by Danny. He designs the sets, among other things. We were rather pleased with his performance at the market. You'll meet him again before long."

"But how did he turn up in Oxbourne?"

"With Charity. She's Bert's sister. She goes to see him at Milton Lodge."

Faith, Hope, Charity and Bert. Of course, Charity reminded him of Bert. "So Bert was involved in this too?"

"Reluctantly. He needed some persuasion. We were a bit worried whether he could pull it off."

Colin took another biscuit and said, "I don't understand how you got involved with this lot in the first place. Or why, if it comes to that. How is this helping your career?"

"It's helping *me*. Listen. I was sick of the endless touring, a few days here, a few days there, packing and unpacking, always on the move. And my so-called career wasn't getting anywhere in any case. I just wanted to stop, have some stability, have some time to take stock. I was in Sanderling a year or two ago."

"With the Enigma. *Much Ado*. Ken Westow spoke highly of your Hero."

Bryony smiled weakly. "You're as good a detective as we thought you would be. I was walking along the beach wondering how I could face another performance when I bumped into Charity. I knew her from the sale of Milton Lodge. That's how we got talking. She arranged for me to meet Sir. It sounded like what I needed. So after the last performance at the church hall I was picked up and brought here."

"Ken Westow said you left pretty abruptly. Upset a few people too."

"I needed to get away. Goodbyes would just have made things more difficult."

"Seems to me you've had more than enough time out of circulation to sort yourself out. How much longer are you proposing to stay here?"

"I'm not sure. I've got a bit of a stake in the place now."

"What sort of stake?"

"I let Sir have some money. To help out at a difficult time. We called it a loan but I can't see him being able to pay it back."

"What on earth for? Why throw your money away on this bunch of losers? Howard Desmond is completely off his head."

"Keep your voice down."

"Why? Are there hidden microphones as well as cameras around the place?"

"Don't get on the wrong side of Sir. He could…he said you had been…uncooperative when you arrived. He thought you might try to leave us."

Too right, thought Colin. What is it with people here? Have they failed to grasp that I'm being held against my will or don't they care? Even Bryony seems to have lost all sense of what constitutes normal behaviour. So much for a damsel in distress. He said, "I'll give it a go. But I'm out of practice. I haven't been near a stage since I left St George's.

"Don't let me down, Col."

Eleven

*W*elcome, welcome. Sit ye down, sit ye down."

Howard Desmond was smiling benignly at the head of a table formed by pushing together six smaller tables distributed haphazardly around the rehearsal room. He gestured towards empty chairs as members of the cast drifted in, paper cup in hand. It was a plain, utilitarian space, windowless and low-ceilinged, huddling in the angle between the theatre and the passage running along the back of the house. The room had a tight, close atmosphere that made Colin feel uncomfortable. He took the chair nearest the door.

"Not positioning yourself for a quick get-away, I trust, young Colin?" Colin flushed and muttered something intended to be reassuring. Tim and Tom giggled nervously and crossed their legs. At the other end of the table, Bryony looked away and stared at the cover of her script.

"Charity is attending to other business so Ted here

will take notes on one of his apparently inexhaustible supply of repulsive yellow pads. I can't think where he gets them, or why for that matter." Ted tapped his pen against a forehead beaded with moisture and smirked unpleasantly.

As Cornelia Thrupp and the mousy girl skittered in apologetically to take the last two places, the old actor closed his eyes momentarily, took a deep breath and raised a copy of the script.

"What do I hold in my right hand?"

"The play, Sir," said Clarence Foible, languidly, after an awkward silence. He was doodling on the back of his rehearsal schedule. Colin had a dim recollection that he had seen a younger model of Clarence on television some years ago in repeats of repeats of 1970s' sitcoms. Could his thick fair hair still be natural?

"Wrong, Malvolio. *We* create the play. These are mere words, marks on paper. What are the words without the actor to give them life? They are our raw material, aids to interpretation, a starting point for our performance. Add to that the sets, the lights, the props, the costumes, the make-up…"

"What about the audience?" said Colin. "Don't they complete the process? I mean, there's not much point without them. Otherwise, we'd just be talking to ourselves."

Celerity Box looked prim, others merely embarrassed.

"Feste has fair point," said Desmond. "In the theatre, we share our thoughts, our performance with the audience, give them something to think about and take away with them. We look to their '*imaginary puissance*' to bridge the gap between word and image. Shakespeare knew that and let the Chorus say so in *Henry V*. At Kemble Place, we improvise to some extent to create the effect we need. As you shall see, my boy."

During the read-through, Desmond remained in apparent good humour. If he was irritated at the inability of certain cast members to keep up, or at the talent of Jack Naseby, playing Sir Andrew Aguecheek, for drying even with the book in front of him, he did not to show it. Colin was struck by the variety of approaches to the task in hand: Vincent Kemp, as Orsino, already word-perfect and bursting with ideas about the role, his costume and the design of the ducal palace; Cornelia Thrupp as Fabian and Clarence Foible as Malvolio, apparently reading the lines for the first time and with all the animation of a station announcer; Tim and Tom playing Sebastian and Antonio with accents of their own devising so thick as to be incomprehensible. They were gently persuaded to drop their attempt at verisimilitude in favour of letting the words speak for themselves. Others, like Bryony, Celerity Box, and Howard Desmond himself, were clearly familiar with the text but appeared reluctant, at this early stage, to give even the hint of a performance.

Colin delivered his lines matter-of-factly and was relieved that he was not yet expected to sing. As the read-through progressed, he was aware of people relaxing, of ice breaking. By the end of it, there was a sense of quiet enthusiasm among the cast, of wanting to make the thing work. It would be all too easy to get drawn in. It was going to be hard, he reflected, to play along and be accepted as a member of the group while remaining detached and ready to take his chance. He had no intention of staying any longer than he had to.

He lay on his bed, staring out of the window. The moon and stars lay behind a veil of cloud. The grounds below were dark and still. On the distant horizon, a smudge of light revealed a fishing boat or some other craft free to come and go. He felt the burden of his isolation and confinement, as if he had been held here for months. Yet it was barely forty-eight hours since he had been downing lager outside the church hall in Sanderling. There was no alcohol to be had at Kemble Place. Not, at least, for lowly players; Howard Desmond and Celerity Box he had seen, with glass in hand, at the Enigma cast party only the night before last. Nor was there any sign of newspapers, radio, television, apart from the monitor in the stable block.

He resolved to draw up a plan of house and grounds and plot the position of cameras and other security devices, noting any potential weak spots or anything else – an overhanging tree, a ladder left out – that might be put to good use. All of which begged the question of Bryony. He was only here because of her, driven by a need to find her, rescue her, convinced that she was being held against her will. Underpinned perhaps by the thought that they might, after all, relive some of the happier, more complicit times they had once had together. And there wasn't anyone else, just at the moment. But any youthful feelings re-kindled had been doused by the realisation that she had tricked him, played an elaborate game to draw him into a trap. She had even taken the photographs herself. And if he had hoped she might still feel anything for him he was rapidly disabused.

He turned over and sighed, more in sorrow than anything else. He lacked the energy for the justifiable anger and resentment at having been used and ending up the captive himself. One thing was plain. He could not trust her. Her loyalty was to Howard Desmond and the group, not to him and memories of their past together. They were different people now. If he shared his plans to escape she would inevitably give him away. If he went, he went alone. In the meantime, he would have to work with her as best he could and keep his thoughts to himself.

Colin declined a second game of Monopoly after supper and said he was going back upstairs. He had only joined at the insistence of Jack Naseby, making up a foursome at the circular table in the corner of the sitting room with Cornelia Thrupp and Brenda, the mousy girl. It was the room off the hall he had found in darkness that first morning at Kemble Place. Other maroon-clad figures were sitting on settees, lounging in armchairs, reading, talking or playing cards.

Jack, taking to his role as banker with exaggerated

care, regaled the assembled company with an apparently inexhaustible fund of anecdotes about his life in the theatre.

"When I was ASM-ing in Frinton, I put on the 'National Anthem' instead of the sound of horses' hooves. The whole audience stood and sang 'God Save the Queen' in the middle of Act One."

Colin moved his boot to Vine Street and bought two houses.

"Another time, I was painting over the flats for the new show, banishing the wooden panelling of the courtroom scene in the last production ready for Regency stripes for the elegant Kensington drawing room in the next one. The flats had been repainted so often they were beginning to crack. Anyway, I'd got into my stride and was singing to keep my spirits up: 'I've Got a Lovely Bunch of Coconuts', as it happens. Our esteemed director, Rex Capon, appears from nowhere and says, for all the world to hear, 'It is a matter of indifference to me, Mr Naseby, whether they're standing in a row, dancing a jig or waiting for a number three bus. I'll thank you to keep the noise down.'

Cornelia collected £100 from each of the other players and added the notes to her pile.

"I was nervous as a kitten on first nights in weekly rep. One Monday evening I ran to the sink as usual and was sick all over the leading lady's piece of haddock. She'd put it there for safe keeping, or so she thought. She wasn't best pleased…"

Brenda fetched up in Free Parking and squeaked.

"Dorothy Lane, her name was. She got on badly with the leading man and, after he accused her of cutting in with lines too soon and killing his laughs, they refused to speak to each other. Communication was by means of notes, which made life difficult all round. Mind you, she had a friendly daughter, an obliging girl called Rita. Very obliging. That made up for a lot."

Colin threw a double five and went forward to Piccadilly.

"I was in the green room at Leatherhead years ago with Ralph Mutton. It was a hot evening after the show and we'd both had a few. Old Ralph spied some girls from the cast heading our way, stood up and declaimed, 'Consider the fillies, how they glow.'"

Cornelia was stung for Luxury Tax between Park Lane and Mayfair.

"Jonquil McCreadie came up to him and said, 'The trouble with you, Ralph, is that you don't take women seriously.' Quick as a flash, old Ralph replied, 'On the contrary, my dear, I'm always serious when I take a woman.' He gave a devilish laugh and furled imaginary moustaches. Good old Ralph. Dead now, of course."

Brenda mortgaged Leicester Square and burst into tears.

Colin's footsteps on the uncarpeted stairs echoed round the hall and stairwell, clumping, harsh and intermittently squeaky. He slowed down and resorted to tip-toe in an effort to deaden the sound. For some reason, he felt guilty, as if creeping back after hours, trying to avoid being caught. As he reached the first-floor landing, he relaxed and resumed his normal posture.

Once again, he was struck by the portraits of varying quality clinging to the walls. He could not decide whether this was a random collection of individuals designed to fill the space above the panelling or represented successive generations of the family of the previous owner. It seemed more likely that the pictures had been bought with the house than accumulated later. As far as he could see, they bore no resemblance to Howard Desmond or Celerity Box themselves. Indeed, the couple appeared to have no family of their own; the websites he had consulted were silent on the matter of children. Perhaps the Kemble Players were some sort of substitute. But surely other cast members must have people who missed them, wondered where they were? How could they drop out of circulation so comprehensively? And what about Aurelia and the other resident staff? Their focus seemed entirely inward, largely oblivious of the outside world.

He paused in front of a picture of an Edwardian gentleman, bewhiskered, portly, stomach straining at the buttons of the waistcoat visible beneath his ample jacket of dogtooth tweed. The victim, no doubt, of spectacular breakfasts and inadequate exercise. The watery grey eyes looked distant, melancholy, those of a thin man failing to get out, unaware of the camera high on the opposite wall.

As Colin turned to climb to the second floor, he heard a cough in the corridor stretching away to his left. The end was lost in gloom. He called as best his dry throat would allow. There was no reply, no sound at all but that of a softly closing door. He took a few steps down the corridor, its wooden floor relieved by rugs placed at irregular intervals. He could just make out a series of doors along both sides. He proceeded cautiously, careful to walk on the rugs, not on the bare boards in between, taking comfort in the thought that if it was difficult for him to see it must be equally hard for him to be seen.

The panelled doors appeared to be identical and were unmarked. There were no names or numbers, no indication of those who lived behind them. No lights showed beneath any of the doors, no sound came from any of the rooms. He reached the end of the corridor, indicated by the dark shape of a cabinet with chairs set squarely on either side, a tapestry of some sort above. As he went back towards the staircase, he heard a noise, more whimpering than crying, coming from a room roughly half way down the corridor. A couple of slaps, followed by the words 'Not yet' in a strong, clear male voice, then silence.

Colin did not linger outside the room or stop until he came to the landing on the second floor. He did not recognise the voice and had no idea who occupied that room or others on the corridor. He knew that Charles and Frank had accommodation at the top of the stable block. That was as far as his knowledge went. He assumed that the Desmonds had a reasonably spacious flat or suite somewhere in the house but was unsure where. The views were better higher up but it did not seem likely, given their age, that they would clamber so far; perhaps there was a lift he had not yet found. He did not even know, and had not asked, where Bryony had her room.

So who had he heard on the other side of the door? He could rule out Jack, Cornelia and Brenda, still at the table when he left the sitting room, and Vincent Kemp, cajoled into taking his place. He struggled to remember the others remaining in the room: Tim and Tom, perhaps, and the effete duo playing Orsino's gentleman attendants, Valentine and Curio, whose names he had failed to grasp.

Little the wiser, he took the narrow staircase that snaked up to the galleried area outside his own room. At the top, he was about to push through the velvet curtain when he saw that the door marked PRIVATE, normally locked shut, was open and a light on in the room beyond. He stood stock-still and listened. He moved close to the entrance, then closer, rehearsing what he would say if someone appeared. He tapped gently on the door, not because he wanted to attract anyone's attention but to give the impression, if there was someone already there, that he was not snooping, just interested.

There was no reply. The room was unoccupied. Yet surely whoever had been here would be back soon. He took in the room as quickly as he could. It was a small windowless space, with a battered desk and swivel chair, flanked by four-drawer filing cabinets in dull battleship grey of the sort often to be seen cluttering pavements outside junk shops and other sellers of redundant furniture. The lack of computer, telephone or other equipment suggested that the room was used mainly for storage rather than as an office.

The cabinet drawers bore pithy but unexciting labels on the lines of 'Insurance', 'Utilities', 'Taxation'. Colin was more interested in the box files ranged against the wall on top of the desk. The spine of each said 'Actors', followed by one or more letters of the alphabet. He was tempted to see whether he had turned up in 'M to P' but took the logistically simpler course of opening the file already lying on the desk. It was 'D to F'.

The file contained a number of buff folders, each with the name of an actor stencilled in the top right-hand corner. He worked his way quickly from the back. Clarence Foible, he knew; Brenda Farrow must be the mousy girl; Terence Edgar, he now recalled, was Curio. But who was James Dudley?

A black-and-white photograph clipped to the left-hand side of the folder showed an actor with dark curly hair looking much the same age as Colin himself, though how long ago the picture had been taken he could not tell. He did not recognise him. On the right-hand side, a plastic wallet laid loosely on top of other papers contained press cuttings. The words 'body' and 'beach' caught his eye as the clunk of heel on stair reached his ears. Someone was on the floor below.

He shoved the wallet inside his tracksuit top, put the folder back in the box file, and left the room. He was through the curtain just as Charity Wise rounded the bend holding a mug of tea at which she gazed intently, possibly in the forlorn hope that she would not spill it. At any rate, she seemed unaware that Colin had seen her momentarily though the gap between curtain and arch before he ambled past the butterfly cabinets to the door of his room. It would not do to rush now that he was back in a region of camera surveillance.

He unfolded the cuttings and spread them on the bed. They were neatly snipped and labelled with the name of the relevant newspaper and its date of issue. They had all appeared within the space of a few days some months earlier. National or local, they all told much the same story, the most detailed account being that in the *Sanderling Recorder*. The body of a young man had been found by an early-morning dog-walker washed up on the beach under the pier at Dotterel a few miles along the coast. The body was clothed but there was nothing to indicate the identity of the deceased. No wallet, credit cards, mobile phone. Non-committal remarks were attributed to the local police and reference made to the likelihood of an inquest but there were no later reports of the outcome.

Presumably, thought Colin, the man on the beach was James Dudley. Why else would the cuttings be in his folder? His identity was obviously known within Kemble Place but it was unclear whether people outside had made the connection. Certainly, no one in Sanderling had mentioned the incident in connection with the house or with Howard Desmond himself. And it did not look as though James had been wearing his tracksuit when he had been found. The newspapers just referred to jeans and tee-shirt.

Had Charity been alluding to him when she said that the person who had abused the privilege to come and go was 'no longer with us'? More to the point, what about Bryony's comment that 'We needed to find a replacement for someone who left us sooner than expected'? Had he, Colin, been lured to Sanderling to take the place of someone who had died in unexplained circumstances? And where did that leave him if he was judged to be less cooperative than they had hoped or required?

Colin felt the fear creep over him as he grasped the true nature of his predicament. He was not just a prisoner. His life was in danger. He had to get out.

Twelve

The wind moaned in the chimney, insistent, penetrating, like the cry of an animal in pain. Debris fell into the hearth, scattering onto the dark boards beyond. The windows rattled and shook, pounded by successive waves of rain, thrumming as if small stones were being sprayed against the glass.

" '*Rough winds do shake the darling buds of May*'," said Vincent Kemp. "We're in for a bumpy ride." His thick slab of moussaka wobbled and collapsed as he brought his plate down with a crash on the refectory table.

"It's still April," squeaked the mousy girl through a mouthful of salad.

"Shakespeare was referring to the tree, not the month, was he not?" said Jack Naseby.

"Opinion is divided on the point," said Howard Desmond. "I have always understood it to be the tree myself."

"What tree is that?" asked Ted Gowanus, removing

his steamed-up glasses and wiping them on a remnant of paper napkin torn from the waistband of his tracksuit.

"Hawthorn, dear," said Cornelia Thrupp. "Don't you have them in Prospect Park, or wherever it was you used to loiter?"

"I don't think Ted was looking at the trees," said Clarence Foible.

"People in glass houses," said Celerity Box, taking a spoon to her blackcurrant sorbet.

"Enough," said Desmond. The table went quiet. "Let us we move on to coffee before we block the next scene."

Colin let the others clamber ahead of him to the mugs and jugs on the table at the side. He took his time, sitting, listening to the wind and the rain. It was curiously satisfying in a mournful sort of way. He watched the stretching and pouring and stirring only a few feet away, the clink of spoon on mug and the banter of the Kemble Players increasingly lost to the gathering storm.

Against his expectations, this apparently dysfunctional group was coming together as a cast rather well. Day by day, they grew in confidence and competence, authority and credibility. As Olivia, Celerity Box, surely, he thought, at least twice the age of Vincent, underwent a startling process of rejuvenation that made it possible to believe she was indeed the object of Orsino's affection. Bryony's assured performance as Viola, consistent with what Ken Westow had said about her role as Hero in *Much Ado*, made it even harder for Colin to understand why she had not progressed further in her career. He and Bryony maintained a cordial relationship, friendly but nothing more.

Danny, the man in the red baseball cap, turned up with a model of the set previously agreed with the director. It reminded Colin of a glimpse of an Ottoman court, similar to the sort of watercolours produced by nineteenth-century travellers he had seen in books in his father's study. A curt nod from Danny passed for acknowledgement that he and Colin had met before.

Members of the cast with smaller parts were deputed to help him construct and paint the set, drawing on the stock of flats and backdrops stored behind the stage. Occasionally, he looked in on rehearsals to sketch the proceedings, pinning the results to the large cork board he had fixed to the wall of the rehearsal room. The delicate drawings of Bryony, of which Colin felt there were a disproportionate number, bore little resemblance to the gaunt and harrowing portrait faked for the purposes of the Oxbourne Thursday market.

After the initial embarrassment of having to sing, Colin was settling into the part of Feste and was not found wanting by Howard Desmond or other members of the cast. Bryony, he knew, was pleased, relieved, that he was joining in with apparent good grace. Increasingly, he began to feel a member of the group. That was what worried him. Lack of contact with the outside world and total focus on activity within the walls of Kemble Place was having an effect, despite his early resolve to remain apart. He had to avoid falling in with what was happening here and passive acceptance of the unacceptable. He was determined to maintain his grip on reality and with it his will to escape.

The wind and rain did not relent. From his room on the top floor, the sea was lost to view, sky and water merged in the grey gloom beyond the thrashing pines. He stood by the window, staring through the spattered glass until the day finally faded to deepest charcoal and there was nothing to see but his own reflection.

Morning brought the sun, pale and bleary through a thin gauze of cloud. Parting the curtains, he saw the grounds below strewn with twigs and broken slates, plastic flower pots and empty buckets. A length of trellis, with climbing rose attached, flapped helplessly by the gate leading to the stable yard. Beyond the wooded area and the thick yew hedge, a tree had blown over and rested against the top of the boundary wall. Could it be? He grabbed his plan. Yes! It was the dead elder on the far side of the glasshouse where he had met Bryony. The excitement mounted within him. This was his chance; he was going to take it.

He had to move quickly before the first bell of day alerted the others to the imminence of breakfast. Sticking to the regulation tracksuit might just reduce suspicion if he met anyone. He was uncertain whether the CCTV screen would be monitored at this hour. He would have to leave his own clothes, watch and mobile phone behind but it was a small price to pay.

He closed the door softly and made his way

downstairs, curbing his instinct to run. He drew the bolts of the garden door at the back of the hall and half-walked, half-jogged down the side of the theatre. He slowed as came into the open and took the brick path away from the house. He realised that he had no money with him, no cards or any form of identification. These too had been handed over when he arrived at Kemble Place. No matter. He could hardly go back and ask for them. He had not thought through what he would do once he was in Sanderling or how he would get to Oxbourne. Go to the police perhaps or seek help at the Mermaid.

Past the glasshouse, just a little further, and he was there. The dead elder, partially uprooted, supported by the wall which had broken its fall. A branch was crushing the razor wire at the top. All he had to do was climb the trunk, leaning at a fairly gentle angle, scramble through the branches, and jump down on the other side.

It was easier said than done. The trunk was wet and slippery and rejected his attempts to find a footing. He tried crawling, inching his way up on hands and knees. This was more effective but painful and slow. Nearly there. Just one more push. The lower branches were within reach when he heard a voice.

"Well, well, well."

"Three holes in the ground."

"That's two more than we need for Mr Mallory, is it not, Frank?"

"I cannot fault the arithmetic, Charles."

"We're disappointed, Mr Mallory."

"Very disappointed."

"Mind you, we like a good escape film."

"*The Wooden Horse.*"

"*Midnight Express.*"

"*The Count of Monte Cristo.*"

Colin struggled to grasp a branch but found his progress impeded by Frank, one foot on the tree, the other on the aluminium ladder he had placed against the wall.

"Or perhaps *Papillon* would be more up Mr Mallory's street. Given his interest…"

"In butterflies…"

"And moths."

"But Kemble Place is the wrong location."

"Quite the wrong location."

Colin hit out, tried to push Frank off the tree. He had to get away; he couldn't fail now. "You're not keeping me here," he shouted. It came out hoarse and strained. But he slipped as he stood up and fell heavily against the trunk, grazing shin and elbow. He clung to the tree, unable to move forward or back.

"I suggest you let us help you down, Mr Mallory," said Charles.

"And come back to the house with us," said Frank.

"It would be the best way."

"The only way."

"Sir is not going to be pleased."

"Indeed he is not."

"He will have to decide what to do with you."

"Your fate is in his hands."

Defeated and demoralised, Colin could think of nothing more to say. He felt crushed by disappointment, fearful of what was to follow. He was led back through the grounds, Charles in front, Frank behind with the ladder. He was cold, tired and hungry and his limbs ached. It began to rain.

Aurelia was waiting at the foot of the stairs with a mug of tea and a clean tracksuit. "There's a first-aid kit in your bathroom cabinet if you need it," she said softly. She turned away quickly and went down the kitchen passage. As Colin began his painful plod to the top floor, the door of the dining room opened a crack. The pale, drawn face was Bryony's. She looked as though she had been crying.

Charles left him at the door of his room.

"I'll come back shortly, Mr Mallory. Sir will be waiting for you in the library."

Thirteen

---

*C*harles opened the library door but remained outside. Colin eased his way to the chesterfield and sat down opposite the winged armchair. It was empty, the space illuminated by the standard lamp to one side. A small leather-bound volume of Browning's verse lay on the tripod table nearby, the place marked by a thin red ribbon. It was fraying at the end. The rest of the room was largely lost in shadow, the windows covered by heavy blinds to protect the books from unwelcome sunlight.

The clunk of a door on the far side signalled the entrance of Howard Desmond. He moved slowly, almost mechanically, like a wind-up toy whose key was about to stop turning. He looked older, thought Colin, bent and shrivelled, as if the body found it hard to bear the weight of his enormous head. Yet, as he took his place in the light of the lamp, he snapped into life and assumed the attitude of taut authority with which Colin was only too familiar.

"Is there anything that you wish to say?" asked Desmond.

Colin shook his head and stared at the floor.

"I had high hopes of you. Bryony was not wrong about your talents. Your Feste was coming along well. It is a pity that you chose to play the fool off-stage too. I do not care to be trifled with."

Colin remained silent.

"I find myself in a dilemma. On the one hand, your removal would be a waste and seriously disrupt preparations for our play. On the other, I cannot let disloyalty and disobedience pass unpunished. So what am I to do? My wife advocates a hard line whereas young Bryony pleads clemency, thinks I should give you a second chance. The trouble is, what guarantee do I have that you will not try to jump ship again? If not now, in a month, six months, a year. There will always be that suspicion, damaging the morale and dynamics of the group. One rotten apple. You know the rest."

"Is that what James Dudley was? A rotten apple?"

"The detail need not concern us. Suffice to say, the warning was there to be heeded. You failed to do so."

"Warning or threat?"

"We are not here to play with words. Whatever course I adopt will put everyone else here to some inconvenience..."

"Oh, yes? And what about my convenience? I was tricked into coming to Kemble Place and held against my will. That's pretty inconvenient for me and presumably illegal."

"Reason not the need. We went though all this when you joined us. Let us cut to the chase. You represent an investment, to strengthen and develop our company and help sustain it in the longer term. I am reluctant to throw away the time and effort without one more attempt to persuade you that cooperation is the way forward. To that end, you will be out of circulation for a little while, to give you the opportunity to reflect on the consequences of maintaining your present line. I trust that you are not averse to your own company?"

"What do you mean?"

"We shall be providing alternative accommodation for you. Somewhat less spacious than your present quarters. How long you are there is up to you."

Howard Desmond reached for the embroidered bell-pull by the fireplace.

"You're not going to lock me in some sort of cell?" He felt the panic rise. "I can't be locked up. I have to have space. Who the hell do you think you are? You simply can't treat people like this."

"I detect a degree of resistance. Yet the remedy is in your own hands. Think on it. I shall receive regular progress reports."

Charles and Frank entered the library and stood behind the chesterfield. Desmond gave them a brief nod.

"Go with them. And remember what I have said."

Colin struggled and kicked out as Charles and Frank took hold of him with some force.

"Careful, boys. I don't want him damaged. Not yet."

*

They took him across the deserted hall and down the kitchen corridor in the direction from which he had come that first night. His instinct was to shake them free and run. But their grip was too tight and he had nowhere to go.

"We all have our parts to play, Mr Mallory. Even me and Frank. We know what's expected and we get on with it. It's simpler that way. It doesn't do to rock the boat."

As the passage narrowed, he let go of Colin's arm and walked ahead. Frank fell in behind, remaining silent. They stopped outside a door within sight of the exit to the stable yard. Charles produced a large black key and turned it sharply in the lock. A short flight of stairs, running parallel to the passage, took Colin and his keepers to a damp and musty area partly below ground level. It was divided into three small rooms, each with a door bolted from the outside.

The middle room contained bed and table and nothing else but a square of carpet in the middle of the uneven brick floor.

"Welcome to your new home, Mr Mallory."

"You aren't seriously going to leave me here?"

"We have our instructions. All being well, your stay will be a short one. Your meals will be brought to you. You will be escorted periodically to the wc off the kitchen corridor, where there is also a small basin for your ablutions. I'll come back with your toilet bag and a bucket for...night-time and emergency purposes."

"Any chance of some food now? I haven't eaten today."

Charles hesitated. "I'll see what I can do."

A dull scrape of bolt and he was alone. He sank on to the bed and did not move. He felt the walls advance towards him, hemming him in. He became breathless, mouth dry, body drenched in sweat. He wanted to shout, scream but no sound would come.

A high window offered a small rectangle of relief. By standing on the table, he could just see through the barred and grubby glass, set a little above the level of the cobbled yard. A hint of jasmine, bricks of a wall, tyres of a car. It was not much but it made the prospect of his confinement marginally less unbearable.

He shook open the tartan blanket folded at the end of the bed and arranged it over him. It reminded him of the one they used to spread in woodland clearings, on springy downland turf, on smooth seaside pebbles, handing round cold sausages, hardboiled eggs, ham sandwiches meticulously pre-quartered in a stack on the breadboard before setting off. It was still there, at twenty-six Mafeking Avenue, biding its time in the blanket box on the landing.

When would he see number twenty-six again? He would be on the way there now, if he had just made it over the wall before the intervention of Charles and Frank. He had no idea when he would get another chance, if he would get another chance. They would be watching him even more closely than before, always assuming that he was let out of his present cell at some point.

He was losing track of time, of how long he had been cooped up at Kemble Place. He struggled to remember how much he had told Clare. She knew about Sanderling in general terms but not that he had made a last-minute decision to go there to see *The Tempest*. Neither, he suspected, had he ever mentioned Howard Desmond. Nothing, in fact, to connect him with this house at all.

He lay back with his head on the one misshapen pillow, trying to avoid putting weight on his grazed and smarting elbow. The pillow was beginning to leak the small cubes of foam, pink and green, with which it was inadequately stuffed. He followed the progress of a spider for some minutes, up the back wall, across the ceiling, to the point where it met the front wall, veiled with gently floating cobweb.

After a while his breathing eased, became more regular. The combination of pale grey ceiling and walls and light from the window, such as it was, made the room seem less oppressive, made him feel less confined. But then a thought struck him. What would happen when darkness fell? There was a light bulb suspended above him, hooded in its dusty metal shade, but no switch in the room itself. When would it be turned on? Surely they would not leave him locked up in the dark? They would not do that, would they?

He remained motionless beneath the blanket for a while, then yawned and twisted, shuffled to get comfortable. He had been set a test but he had no idea what he had to do to pass. What signs or symptoms were supposed to represent compliance or sufficient progress to be allowed out? He could say anything they liked to sound cooperative but they knew as well as he did that he would never really be trusted. Perhaps they relied on the example of James Dudley to keep him in check second time round. A warning to be heeded, Howard Desmond had said, apparently unsurprised that Colin had known about the missing actor to begin with.

He yawned again, louder and longer. If he had a book, it would help. There was nothing, no reading matter of any description, apart from barely decipherable washing instructions on the bed clothes. What did prisoners do in situations like this? Count to a million? Recite poems learned at school? Do endless press-ups? Or did they make model ships out of bones left over from meals, like Napoleonic prisoners of war?

None of the above appealed in any event. He recalled the words of Bottom that had come to him outside the donkey shop in Sanderling:

> '*I will walk up and down here, and I will sing, that they shall hear I am not afraid.*'

His pacing was severely constrained by the size of the room and the presence of table and bed. He tipped the table on to the bed and rolled up the carpet for good measure. It helped, but not much. He proceeded as briskly as circumstances would allow and found himself singing 'The Grand Old Duke of York' over and over again. It must have been louder than he realised.

"Delighted that you are in such fine voice, Mr Mallory," said Charles, entering with a tray balanced on the palm of his left hand. Colin had not even heard the bolt being drawn. "It was much enjoyed in the kitchen." He set the table on the floor and slid the tray on top. "Aurelia has prepared a little something for you," said Charles, deftly removing the aluminium lid of a plate heaped with one of her celebrated cooked breakfasts. "She said she had catered for you anyway and it wouldn't do to let it go to waste." Colin let loose a half-smile; the meal had clearly just been cooked for him and the pot of coffee freshly brewed.

"Thanks," he said, not wishing to appear too effusive. "I could get used to room service."

Charity arrived that first afternoon, startling him with light as she flicked the switch on the outside. She took in the room swiftly and silently and returned with a chair that wobbled on the uneven floor.

"Well," she said, looking disconcertingly Bertish as she shifted in her seat. "I'm told that you're unaccountably cheerful, all things considered."

"I was moved to song in a weak moment."

"The question is, how long do you wish to remain here?"

"At Kemble Place?"

"In this room."

"No longer than I have to. The remedy is in my

own hands, according to Howard Desmond. Pity he didn't say what it was."

"Sir is looking for a more positive attitude."

"And how am I supposed to demonstrate that locked up in a cell?"

"On the basis of chats such as this one and other reports reaching my ears."

"The decision is yours?"

"No. My job is to recommend. Sir will decide, no doubt after another interview with you."

"When might that be?"

Charity paused. "It all depends. Sir will need to be convinced that you're serious about staying with us. He's not going to believe you've changed heart overnight or that the odd day or two's detention would represent adequate punishment for what he sees as disloyalty. And don't forget Celerity Box."

"What about her?"

"The *éminence blonde*. Sir won't do anything without consulting her. She will need convincing too."

"Is that where James Dudley went wrong?"

Charity flushed. "You're a better actor. Remember that."

It was worst in the early hours, alone in the dark, curled under the blanket as the walls closed in. The light was turned off after his final escorted visit down the corridor, the delivery of a swift 'good night', and the cold metallic scrape of the bolt rammed home. He was determined to maintain the veneer of calm and good humour for as long as he could; he would not give them the pleasure of seeing the torment and sheer boredom of his confinement.

Whatever it was he thought he would be doing in his mid-twenties, it was not this. Incarcerated among a bunch of losers and eccentrics – two or three times his age, many of them – apparently lacking any control over their own destinies or the desire to do other than follow the course set for them by the monstrous duo. He was paying the penalty for frittering freedom while he still had it, for drift and not having a clear vision about what he wanted. Perhaps that was not so unusual, even if most of his Harvard contemporaries seem to have had jobs lined up, careers mapped out, in legal, political, corporate worlds that held no interest for him. Still, drift was one thing, the sheer recklessness that had landed him at Kemble Place was quite another. He heard the voice of Clare over his shoulder, chiding him gently. Or not so gently. He had to get back to Oxbourne as soon as he could; he had to get a grip and make it happen.

Yet again he found himself asking how, why, everyone else in the house appeared to accept the autocratic regime of the Desmonds without demur. They knew full well that he had been tricked into coming to Sanderling and was being held against his will. Yet they acted as if his presence at Kemble Place was the most natural thing in the world. Was there something in the water or Aurelia's spiced biscuits? Howard Desmond had hinted that the Kemble Players largely comprised people who wanted to be out of circulation for a while, people for whom isolation from the outside world was a positive advantage. For them, perhaps, the house was a refuge, providing comfort and security, and going along with the bizarre set-up was a small price to pay.

Did that extend to the disappearance and death of James Dudley? He supposed it was possible that, in the absence of newspapers or other media, they had not heard about the body on the beach, just thought he had escaped. And, on reflection, the death could have been an accident; he had no firm proof to the contrary, despite dark hints that he might suffer a similar fate if he refused to fall into line. Was it just a ruse to frighten him into compliance?

He wondered what the other players had to hide, what misdemeanours they themselves might have committed, what past debts they might owe the Desmonds. Bryony apart, he had never sought to ask their motives, to probe their backgrounds, and they showed little interest in his. The focus was on the matter in hand: production of the play.

How far any of this applied to the staff was another matter. Charles, Frank, Aurelia: what were they doing here, what explained their loyalty to the Desmonds? And as for Charity…her daily visits entailed little more than gentle, undemanding and apparently aimless chat. After three or four afternoons, he felt just about comfortable enough to ask her a few questions without jeopardising his own position.

"So, how long have you known Howard Desmond?"

"Oh, we go back many years. To the old Sanderling Rep."

"But you weren't on the stage yourself?"

"Good Lord, no. I couldn't act for toffee. My role has always been behind the scenes. Management, administration, making things happen. I always used to say that if I'm not noticed, it's because things are running smoothly and I'm doing my job."

"But the Rep folded in, what, the 1980s?"

"I stayed on at the Darlington. And when that closed I got work elsewhere on Sir's recommendation. We kept in touch, you see."

"Where does Oxbourne fit into this?"

"That was more Mother and the others. They wanted somewhere smaller after our father died. I never stayed there for any length of time, never called it home. It was just a repository for some of my things. Then Mother died too and Faith and Hope decided to buy a bungalow in Devon on the strength of the money she left them. Bert couldn't bear to move, even though we'd only been there a few years. Shame he's let the place get into such a state; he could easily afford to put it to rights, though you'd never think so to look at him."

"You were already here?"

"I got the call from Sir about three years ago. He said he needed someone he could trust to help him run the Kemble Players, as he called them. I was flattered to be asked and there was nothing much else on the horizon. When I inherited my share of Mother's money a little later, I was pleased to offer him a substantial sum. Running this operation doesn't come cheap and what else did I need it for?"

You too, thought Colin. How many others have parted with cash for the privilege of supporting Howard Desmond and Celerity Box? Yet it only seemed to put them further in thrall to the appalling pair, less able or willing to exercise any critical faculties at all.

Eighteen…nineteen…twenty. He was touching his toes when the familiar rasp of bolt and sigh of door heralded the arrival of Charles bearing breakfast.

"When I come back for the tray, Mr Mallory, I shall take you to your room for a shower and a change of clothing. I think Sir would appreciate it."

Point taken. A week or so in the same clothes and minimal ablutions was becoming pretty noticeable, even to him.

"Am I being set free? Am I?"

"That's a matter for Sir to decide. I shall await further instructions."

"Good morrow, good morrow; welcome, my boy." Howard Desmond was in expansive mood. "Sit ye down, sit ye down."

Colin lowered himself slowly to the chesterfield.

"I have received an assessment, an appraisal. The auguries, it seems, are good."

His right hand, gnarled, liver-spotted, slipped to the tripod table. He raised a copy of *Twelfth Night* roughly to eye-level and said, "What do I hold in my hand?"

"A copy of the book. Not the play."

"Quite so. And why not the play?"

"We make the play; those are merely words."

"Excellent. Are you ready to rejoin us, Feste, to make the play?"

"I'm looking forward to it."

"Then there's not a moment to lose. I suggest you go and reacquaint yourself with your part. You've missed the run-throughs on stage but, judging by your performance in the rehearsal room, I'm prepared to live with that. You still have your notes?"

"I do."

"Splendid. I shall detain you no longer. We assemble after lunch for the technical rehearsal."

His appearance in the dining room was greeted with beams, hugs and a manly shaking of hands. Aurelia, dewy-eyed, insisted on bringing him a plate of lasagne and salad while the others helped themselves.

"I'd say you were missed," said Cornelia Thrupp, pushing Brenda, the mousy girl, on to the bench beside her. "Tim and Tom took it in turns playing Feste. Total disaster. Sir was getting crosser and crosser, wasn't he, my little sparrow?" She stuck a fork hard into the arm of the mousy girl, who squeaked and nodded agreement.

"The odds on your return were shortening by the hour," said Jack, dabbing lasagne from the front of his tracksuit. "My guess was tomorrow but I should have known that Sir would want you back before the tech."

"We're in for simply aeons of tedium," said Cornelia,

"while Ted and Danny fiddle with their equipment, if you'll pardon the expression. Over and over the same old stuff while they adjust a spot here, a spot there, or turn down the volume of the music so the actors can actually be heard." She saw Colin looking round the room. "If you want Little Miss Perfect, she's still in the theatre, playing with those dummies of hers."

He pushed through two sets of double doors and entered the theatre. A burst of taped applause greeted his arrival. It stopped as abruptly as it had started.

"Howdy, stranger." Ted Gowanus waved stiffly from the console installed in the small gallery at the back and turned to sort his lighting gels. The stage was richly set as a room in Orsino's palace; Howard Desmond spurned the practice of some directors of starting Act I with Scene 2. "If the Bard had wanted to begin the play with Viola emerging from a shipwreck he would have done so. His intention was clearly to introduce us to the lovelorn Duke and, through him, to the Countess Olivia, the object of his affections."

What passed for the auditorium was piled with chairs and quantities of dummies in various states of undress and in a variety of poses. Some were traditional tailor's dummies on adjustable poles and wooden tripods. Others were full-scale mannequins, complete with head and complement of limbs. Their fleshly tones were disturbingly life-like. Wigs and clothes, female and male, dripped from bags and boxes like molten Dali watches.

Bryony shuffled in through a door on the other side,

hugging a large black bin-bag stuffed with shoes and handbags. She looked up and smiled broadly. Not at all the pale and drawn face he had seen briefly after he had been led back in from the garden.

" '*What country, friends, is this?* ' "

" '*This is Illyria, Lady.*' "

"Looks more like the church jumble sale at the moment. Col, how are you?" She put the bag with the others and glanced at the gallery. "You've put on weight. I hope you can get into your costume."

"It wasn't exactly a diet of bread and water. Aurelia's been feeding me up, like a Christmas goose."

"But with a happier ending, I hope. Have you met the audience?" She gestured towards the dummies. "They'll be tricked out like proper theatre-goers before we get to dress rehearsal."

"Yes, but…"

"When you're on stage, with the house lights down and Ted's sound effects, you can quite believe they're real."

"Boos, whistles, catcalls?"

"They're far too polite. They stick to applause and laughter; Ted has a script marked up for audience reaction."

"Do you sell them ice-cream and programmes too?"

"Stop it," she said, grinning hugely. "Sir takes this seriously. As we all do."

She looked stunning, even in maroon. He looked away for a moment. Oh, Bryony, Bryony, why are you wasting yourself here?

"Where on earth did you get them, anyway?"

"Junk shops, dress shops closing down, that sort of thing. We had a job lot from Fun Fashions when they moved from the high street. Danny came and picked them up in his van. I got most of the clothes from charity shops."

Like the donkey shop, he thought. With the mousy girl to carry the bags.

"You seem to have been busy. And privileged to keep going into town. Howard Desmond obviously trusts you."

"Yes," she said. "He does."

The tech finished well after supper. Aurelia produced coffee and sandwiches out of nowhere as members of the cast slumped in the sitting room, exhausted but too wound up to contemplate sleep. Colin, wedged uncomfortably between Jack Naseby and Clarence Foible, was hoarse from constant repetition of snatches of song as Ted and Danny made constant adjustments to lighting and sound levels in response to bellowed instructions from the director.

"Well done, people," said Howard Desmond, rising slowly, mug in one hand, cheese and pickle in the other. He looked drained and worn, thought Colin, almost frail.

"Nothing that a bit of padding and a stick of number nine won't cure," whispered Clarence, reading Colin's mind with an accuracy he found troubling. Was he always so transparent?

"It's been a long day," the director continued. "We have achieved much. Dress rehearsal tomorrow and then we open."

"What, no previews?" said Tim.

"Or press night?" said Tom.

"We have no need of the agency of the press to encourage our audience to attend. I am confident of an enthusiastic response and a long run."

Celerity Box led brief but good-humoured applause and the company fell in to quiet consumption and increasing drowsiness from which they were rudely awoken by the sudden intrusion of Charity. Bearing clipboard and expression of pent-up concern, she approached Howard Desmond and invited him to step into the hall for an urgent word. She threw a glance in the direction of Colin and left the room as quickly as Desmond's pace would allow.

A few minutes later he returned, looking grave. He clapped his hands and said, "Time for bed, people. Tomorrow is another day."

Fourteen

The rehearsal room had been turned into a dressing room for the whole company, except Howard Desmond and Celerity Box. They shared the space off the corridor leading from the auditorium that normally accommodated Bryony's dummies and related paraphernalia. The table in the middle of the room was divided lengthways by a double line of mirrors of varying shapes and sizes, placed back to back and illuminated by spotlights set on stands at strategic points. Racks of costumes lined the walls, carefully labelled by character and the scenes in which they were to be worn. Aurelia, acting as wardrobe mistress, was on hand to give advice and ease people in to and out of their clothes.

"Boys on the left, girls on the right," she called as the company trooped in with make-up bags and boxes, collecting their wigs from the table by the door. The division was scarcely necessary as the bank of mirrors offered no privacy at all and people were too busy sorting themselves out to take notice of anyone else. It was also ineffective, as the proportions of male and female cast members led to overcrowding on one side and empty chairs on the other. Tim and Tom volunteered to be girls.

"Why change the habit of a lifetime, dears?"

"You're one to talk."

"Perhaps Cornelia should sit on the boys' side."

"Meaning what, exactly?"

"You're playing Fabian. What did you think I meant?"

The combination of spots and a dozen or so bodies soon made the room unpleasantly hot, the actors' discomfort made worse by the donning of wigs and heavy costumes. Colin, in dress reminiscent of a mediaeval minstrel, complete with knee-length boots and feathered cap, was sitting nearest the door. He was roughly opposite Brenda, whom he glimpsed between mirrors applying powder at a furious rate. The change in her demeanour from down-trodden mousy girl to the spirited Maria struck him as even more remarkable than the transformation of Celerity Box to the Countess Olivia.

He needed to escape the closeness of the room.

"Just going to get some air," he told Aurelia as he opened the door and slipped into the corridor, oblivious to the flash of concern in Bryony's eyes as she rose above the level of her mirror. He could hear music coming from the auditorium. He clopped towards it, a little unsteady in his high-heeled boots. The door of the stars' dressing room, now bearing their names on freshly printed card, was slightly ajar, moving gently in an unfelt draught. He cleared his throat, once, twice. No sound came from the room. He gave the door a surreptitious nudge as he bent to straighten a recalcitrant boot. He saw a large mirror fixed to the wall. It was framed by light bulbs, many of which were working. On the table in front, a pair of vacant wig stands, sticks and jars of make-up, packs of playing cards, a copy of the script. A silk dressing gown was draped over each chair, neatly arranged as if designed to be seen from the outside. The one burgundy, with the initials H.D. picked out in gold on the breast pocket; the other lavender, with C.B. in sparkling silver. And below the table, a cardboard box. It had once contained tins of pineapple chunks, or so it said; now it housed a lighter load of masks similar – no, identical – to the one he had seen part-burnt on the beach.

" '*Alas, poor fool, how have they baffled thee!*' "The words were fired from Celerity Box, in full fig as the Countess Olivia, rounding the corner from the stage door passage. "I like the feather, Feste. It matches your tights. Can we help in any way?"

"I seem to have mislaid my tabor. I'll need it for the second half."

Bryony told Colin after lunch. He was, it seemed, the last person at Kemble Place to hear. The dress rehearsal was over and Howard Desmond declared himself well pleased.

"This promises to be the Kemble Players' finest

production to date. Congratulations, people. We shall have spiced biscuits with our tea."

She led him into the garden. The wooded area beyond the lawn was studded with rhododendrons in flower, crimson, pink and white. He thought wistfully of the ones loose in the woods at home, the same woods he used to roam with Bryony before they went their separate ways. Now they were together again, yet scarcely together at all. He made an effort to catch up as she headed for a bench, silver-grey with age, glistening in the sun that had dried the morning's rain.

In the stable block, there was sudden interest in a flickering television screen.

"Well, look who it is, Frank."

"The stars of the show, I hear, Charles."

"Not forgetting Sir, of course."

"Or his good lady wife."

"Our Mr Mallory is said to be a reformed character."

"A valued member of the team."

"After his brief incarceration."

"His period of confinement."

"But do leopards change their spots, I wonder?"

"Or merely cover them with grease paint?"

"Time will tell."

"Indeed it will."

"But he hasn't been told yet, has he?"

"I rather think not."

"It may make a difference, Charles."

"We shall be watching, Frank."

When they had both sat down, Bryony said, "There's

something you need to know." Her face was drawn, unsmiling. "You're bound to find out sooner or later so I thought I'd better tell you. Sir agrees."

"You're sounding very mysterious. And what is our director's trusty lieutenant authorised to reveal? Is he selling up and moving to a retirement home with his lovely wife? Does this mean disbanding the Kemble Players or is he leaving you in charge?"

"Listen, Col. The situation is this. Charles was in the town yesterday afternoon, picking up provisions for the week ahead. On his way back he stopped at one of the charity shops to collect some clothes they'd been keeping for me."

"Not the donkey shop?"

"Yes. It was. While he was collecting the bags from the back room, two people came in and asked the woman at the cash desk whether they'd seen the man in a photograph they showed her. Apparently, she told them he had come into the shop a few weeks earlier but she had not seen him since and didn't know where he was."

"Do you mean a picture of me? Is someone looking for me?" His mind ran ahead of his tongue, fuelled by a mixture of elation and relief at the prospect of freedom after the failure of his previous attempt to escape.

"Charles couldn't see who was in the photograph but…"

"Who was it, the police? Was it the police?"

"The woman said the person they were after had also been looking for someone in a photograph and asked if this was some sort of game. If so, it was wasting her time."

"Then what?"

"They assured her it was not a game, put some money in her collection box, and left."

"So it *was* me they wanted. But hang on. She clearly remembered you when I was in the shop. If Charles was picking up stuff on your behalf why didn't she call him to come and look at the photograph or get him to tell these people where you were? For all she knew, I might have found you."

"I've no idea. Perhaps she didn't make the connection with Charles at the time."

"Hm. I wonder. So, who were they? Who knows I'm in Sanderling?"

"According to Charles, it was a middle-aged man and a girl, as he put it." Bryony hesitated. "He said they looked a lot like you."

"But that could only be Clare…and Dad." He grinned broadly. "My parents must be back from the States." He stood up suddenly and then sat down again. "Where are they now?"

"I don't know."

"So they could still be here, if they stayed the night."

"I suppose so."

"How did they end up in the donkey shop? They couldn't have known I'd been there."

"I don't know that either. But there's another thing."

"What?"

"Charity had a call from her brother in Oxbourne."

"The flatulent Bert."

"It seems they went to the house and spoke to him."

"He must know I'm here."

"Yes, but I don't think he told them."

"Presumably not or they'd have come straight to Kemble Place. They or the police."

"Charity's worried that Bert may not be so reliable another time."

"Howard Desmond sounded pretty positive at lunch."

"He wants to keep up the company's morale."

"The others already know, I take it?"

"They've heard that someone's been looking for you."

"So much for our director's confidence that I wouldn't be missed."

"Col?" She sounded subdued, forlorn.

"Yes?"

"Whatever happens, let's make the first night a success. That means a lot to all of us."

Fifteen

---

*I*t was Frank who saw it first. Bored with staring at the television screen for hours on end, he had wandered off to make another mug of tea and tackle the crossword. Like the rest of the staff, he was not subject to the ban on newspapers and other forms of contact with the outside world that applied to members of the Kemble Players themselves. Nothing much was likely to be happening now in any event, he thought. The cast and crew were settling down to an early supper before heading for the theatre to prepare for the opening night. He was happy to wait and have something at his usual time.

He sank into the armchair of rust-coloured uncut moquette installed in one corner of the former tack room. The matchboarded walls still bore names painted in black above the empty saddle racks: Good Boy, Stromboli, Rose-Marie, Lucky Star…the names of horses stabled here many years before Howard Desmond and Celerity Box came to the Red House.

Frank lingered longer than he had intended. Six down was proving troublesome, as was nineteen across. He reached for the dictionary, an old and fraying Concise Oxford lurking on the lower tier of the wobbly bamboo table on which he had parked his mug. The dictionary was not the one recommended by the crossword compiler but it was the only one he had, liberated from the library one morning when the house had been largely deserted. 'Escape tax customary north of the border.' Scot free, of course. Only one left. Better get back, though. He could finish the crossword later.

He glanced with little interest at the changing pictures on the screen before him. Their quality, he reflected, seemed worse than ever. Particularly the one showing the area at the top of the house, outside the room allocated to Mr Mallory. It had a grainy, smoky appearance that made it hard to see. Christ! It *was* smoke, seeping, as far as he could tell, from under the door of the room. He needed to get help. Everyone would be in the theatre by now, even Charles who was lending a hand with the scene changes.

As he ran across the courtyard between stable block and house he could smell the smoke, hear the crack of flame. The tower room was ablaze. There was no sprinkler system at Kemble Place and the fire, he could see, was already beyond the capacity of a few extinguishers. He flung open the door to the kitchen corridor and sprinted faster than he had done in years.

*

Colin was lurking in the wings, waiting to go on for his first scene. Brenda, as Maria, gyrated nearby as she made a last-minute adjustment to her costume. He was not concentrating. He had been shaking in the dressing room but laughed it off when people enquired, putting it down to first-night nerves. Jack tried to lighten the mood by repeating his story about being sick over the leading lady's piece of haddock. He was not altogether successful.

Bryony was now on stage as Viola in man's attire, temporarily disguised as Cesario. Colin wondered how much longer he had, how much longer it would be before events took an altogether different course. Apart from Frank, closeted in the stable block, everyone was here. The house itself was empty. As the highest point of Kemble Place, his own room had seemed ideal. It had the best chance of being seen from outside, of drawing an audience more active and useful than a bunch of dummies. It was also the one place he could go by himself without causing suspicion and operate without being seen.

Timing had been his main concern. If he moved too soon the fire would be spotted and put out and the perpetrator would be readily apparent. But he could not leave it much later as he had to get ready for the performance. He would then be with the others for the rest of the evening. In theory, at least.

"Blast," he said, as he was changing into his costume. "I've left my make-up box upstairs," the 'box' being an old ice-cream carton produced by Aurelia to house the sticks of greasepaint he had been given after his rehabilitation.

"Use mine, dear."

"Or mine."

"Thanks, but it's rather a personal thing, make-up. I'm pretty sure I left it on my bed. I'll just nip back and get it. I'm not on for a bit, in any case."

He slipped on his tracksuit bottoms and trainers and dashed away. No self-respecting arsonist would risk laddering his tights or do the deed wearing high-heeled boots, quite apart from the practicalities. Once in his room, he removed the pile from under his bed, the scrumpled sheets of lined yellow paper torn from the pad he had been given to take notes during rehearsal. He arranged them under the part-drawn curtains. He snatched the matches from beneath his pillow, a small box he had palmed from the dining room mantelpiece a couple of days before. He felt sick as he attempted to strike a match and put it to the paper.

After a tentative start, it took little time for the flames to reach the curtains and take a hold. It was a curiously hypnotic process but he had to get back. He pulled the bedside rug sufficiently high against the door to ensure that the gap below would be largely covered when the door was closed. Hardly airtight but it should keep the smoke at bay for a while. He grabbed the make-up box and slipped deftly onto the landing.

He found himself holding the good luck cards that had been sneaked under his door during the day. Apparently, the exchange of such cards among cast members was traditional, even obligatory, on first nights. At least, in the conventional theatre. At Kemble Place, the opportunities for buying them were somewhat limited. 'Here's to a wonderful evening and a successful run.' This in deep violet ink, signed with a flourish 'H.D and C.B.' 'On with the show! Lots of luck, from Jack.' 'Let's strive to please them every day, love B.'

He faltered momentarily. But there was no going back. It had to be done; there was no other way. He felt bad too about leaving his jacket, the bottle-green velvet jacket he had bought in Boston and worn so often that it became his trademark. He could see no way of taking it downstairs, an area where own-clothes were banned, without giving rise to unhelpful questions and further distrust. And it was now too late to throw it out of the window in the hope of retrieving it afterwards.

"Bingo," he said with a nervous laugh, as he banged the box down on the table. "All sticks present and correct."

"We were beginning to wonder where you'd got to."

"Sorry. I stopped to look for some paracetamol. It wasn't where I thought it was."

"Are you all right, love?"

"Just a bit of a headache. You know how it is."

"Well, it looks like being a good house. The place is packed."

They were on. A room in Olivia's house.

Maria: '*Nay, either tell me where thou hast been, or I will not open my lips so wide as a bristle may enter, in way of thy excuse: my Lady will hang thee for thy absence.*'

Clown: '*Let her hang me: he that is well hang'd in this world, needs to fear no colours.*'

Enter Frank through heavy auditorium doors, out of breath, sweating heavily. He crashed into a couple of elegantly dressed mannequins and knocked them to the floor. If they were aggrieved, they did not show it, maintaining expressions of calm collection and haughty detachment despite the loss of their wigs.

"The tower room," gasped Frank. "It's on fire."

According to the following week's edition of the *Sanderling Recorder*, Dave and Margaret Buckley, a retired couple walking their dog along the beach, noticed a glow in the western sky. At first, they had thought it was the dying moments of the very fine sunset that had earlier bathed the shore in warm gold light. They then made out flames leaping above and beyond the pines bordering the property that lay behind a high brick wall. Dave used his wife's mobile phone to alert the fire and rescue service recently relocated to brand new premises on the Dotterel Road. The couple then proceeded back to town as smartly as their dog, their legs, and the clinging sand would allow.

*

Celerity Box and Clarence Foible rushed onto the stage when Brenda squeaked what Frank had said. The premature entrance of Olivia and Malvolio was followed by that of Howard Desmond much bulked-up as Sir Toby Belch. Celerity Box took charge.

"Round up the cast and crew. Find buckets and extinguishers and proceed to the top of the house. Take water from the nearest bathroom."

"But the play," said Desmond. "We must go on."

"With the house burning about our ears? Don't be ridiculous."

"It's more than we can handle," said Frank. "We need to call the fire brigade."

"We can't have outsiders here," said Desmond.

Charity hurried into the auditorium with Charles, Aurelia and the rest of the cast as Ted and Danny turned to leave the gallery.

"Charles," said Celerity Box, "go with Frank and appraise the situation. Quickly."

Charles extracted the front door key from his jacket pocket as the pair ran to the hall. Desmond made to follow them.

"Where are you going?"

"To our rooms. To save our possessions. Our whole lives are there; our memories; everything."

"Not at your age and not with all that padding."

"We could go," shouted Tim and Tom.

"We must all wait here."

Charles returned with Frank limping behind. "It's an inferno," he said. "It's far too big to tackle by ourselves."

Howard Desmond let out a groan.

"Then we have no alternative," said Celerity Box. "Charity: go to the library and telephone the fire brigade."

Charity strode to the hall, still holding her clipboard. She returned almost immediately.

"They're already on their way."

Through the open front door they could hear sirens increasing in volume as two fire engines made their way down Sandy Lane, blue lights flashing.

"Frank: open the gates to let them in. Charles and Danny: go and move the car and van to the far side of the stable yard. The rest of you assemble on the back lawn. That includes you," she said to Desmond. "I shall meet the men at the front door."

As they filed out, Ted said to Colin, "You're one lucky guy. On another day you could have been in the tower room at this time."

"That's a sobering thought," said Colin.

Bryony looked at him but said nothing. She was not the only one who knew that Colin had been back to his room not long before the fire must have started.

The group made its way silently to the far side of the lawn, close to the edge of the wooded area. The garden was lit up by a furiously flickering orange light as the fire gained control of the tower roof. Aurelia dabbed at her eyes with the sleeves of her cardigan; Cornelia put an arm round Brenda, who had reverted fully to her mousy girl persona. Charity raised her clipboard and started to take a roll call. It was hard to hear above the crack and roar of flames and the rumpus coming from the front: the fire engines had arrived and men were moving quickly. Further sirens in the distance suggested that reinforcements were on their way.

"Where's Sir?" asked Jack.

"He was with us when we left," said Clarence.

"He must have gone back inside," said Bryony.

"Perhaps he's with Celerity…Box," said Vincent Kemp, starting to unpeel the beard he was wearing as Orsino.

"No, she's coming down the path. Look," said Ted.

Charles, Frank and Danny crossed the lawn from the stable yard and came to join them. None had seen Howard Desmond. Charity reported the situation to Celerity Box.

"Don't tell me the old fool went back upstairs while I was out the front. I'm not clambering after him in this. I'd better tell the firemen. Charles, will you come with me, please."

Colin took a step towards the woodland shadows.

"Where are you going?" asked Bryony.

" '*I will but look upon the hedge.*' I drank too much water before I went on."

"Use the one in the stable block," said Frank, in a sudden access of generosity. "It's next to the tack room."

This was his chance. He went gently towards the stable yard; once through the gateway he quickened his pace. His plan was to cut round the side to the front and slip out of the open gates. But it was a confusion of light, sound, movement: flashing, throbbing, pulsating, shouting. Water cascaded down the front of the house and flooded the drive. A section of the roof collapsed, sending slate and blackened timbers crashing to the ground. There was no way out.

He retreated to the stable block and made for the office. On the television screen he saw Celerity Box in the hall being encouraged to leave by Charles and men in uniform. She was gesticulating, pointing upwards, shouting words he could not hear. The screen changed to show firemen, equipment on the stairs, the Edwardian gentleman observing the scene with lofty unconcern. Hints of smoke but not much more. The fire itself appeared to be contained on the top floor. Of Howard Desmond there was no sign.

Colin picked through the tattered labels of keys hanging from hooks on the green baize board to the right of the screen. Everything except the one he wanted. He worked his way through them again, left to right, top to bottom. He was beginning to panic; he had been gone too long. Someone was bound to come looking. Yet there was no pattern or sequence to the keys that would provide a clue, a short cut.

Last row. Second hook. Hang on. There were two labels; two sets of keys. One set for the door of the stable that served as a workshop and store room; the other for the back gate to Kemble Place. He grabbed the second set, a pair of shiny Yale keys, and left the room. The back gate was the one he had seen from the other side when he had walked along the beach from the Mermaid. Was that the way Bryony went into town, the reason she had sand in her shoes when she went to the donkey shop? He himself had never seen anyone leave the property by that route.

He heard voices. Two figures were silhouetted in the gateway giving on to the back lawn. They looked like Frank and Charles. He ducked and slipped behind the van parked in the far corner of the stable yard. He skirted van and Daimler and waited until the men were in the stable block. He loitered by the gateway. This was the most dangerous part, the greatest risk of being seen. He crept past the climbing rose, now firmly back in place and severely pruned since his previous escape attempt. With the fire now largely under control, the garden was no longer bathed in orange light and the moon was merely a sliver. But he had to be careful. It was by no means pitch dark and he could clearly see the shifting group on the lawn.

He heard snatches of complaint: they were cold, hungry, thirsty, when could they go back inside? There were subdued references to 'Sir' and then the distant but growing sound of another siren. The group's attention appeared to focus on Celerity Box, now drifting back towards the house. He made for the shadows of the wooded area and, staying low, headed towards the gap in the yew hedge. He was through.

It was a good deal darker beyond the hedge. At first he could make out nothing at all. Then the pale frame of the glasshouse on his left appeared in the murk, high beds of railway sleepers on his right. He stepped tentatively along the path in the direction of the pines.

The siren became louder and louder and then stopped. A moment's silence, then shouting. Different voices, different people, but a single word. They were calling his name.

He hurried forward as best he could, past the remains of the fallen elder, partially dismembered and pulled away from the wall. He had not been this far before. The flash of a torch caught the edge of a fruit cage. Had he been spotted? He broke into a run. His hat tumbled to the ground: he had quite forgotten he was wearing it. He groped to retrieve it and was off, clutching the keys so tightly that they dug into the palm of his hand.

The pitted path was sloping now, down towards the stand of pines. The path became a sandy track, crunchy with debris, snaking between the trees. Another flash lit up the branch above him. He heard his name again, but called in a tone suggesting that he was still being sought rather than having been seen. As far as he could tell, they had not noticed that the keys were missing.

The track veered to left and right and brought him to the solid wooden gate set firm between stone piers. He felt around the gate, stabbing blindly: two bolts, it seemed, both secured by padlocks. And a pull handle. He fumbled to insert a key into the higher padlock. It would not turn. He snatched it out and tried the other key. This time it worked. He removed the padlock and drew the bolt. Another light, two lights, penetrated the pines and struck the top of the wall. He could not judge how close they really were. Now the other padlock, the other bolt. He gripped the handle; the gate scraped towards him.

He did not linger on the worn stone step on the other side. He took off his hat and ran.

Sixteen

It was not easy wearing high-heeled boots, teetering, tottering along the flinty path until he sank into the coarse sand beyond. He felt absurd, grateful that the inadequate moon spared him all but the faintest light, as if anything brighter would expose him to public scrutiny, to ridicule, to gales of raucous laughter. Yet the beach was surely deserted at this hour, dog-walkers and random strollers long returned to hearth, home or the nearest pub. All he could make out, through the indigo haze, was a blurred band of silver-grey shimmering on the surface of the sea.

Of his pursuers, there was neither sight nor sound, not even the flash of a torch. By now, they must have found the gate unlocked and unbolted and pulled roughly open. He had had no means of closing it behind him. Perhaps, given the events of that evening, they had decided their priorities lay within the curtilage of Kemble Place. Or maybe they were intent on intercepting him nearer the town. But with the drive blocked by fire engines it seemed unlikely that they could get there in a hurry.

He was taking no chances. He trudged forward unsteadily, pausing to rest on the steps of the beach huts, shuttered and still, that he had seen on his early morning walk from the Mermaid weeks before. Quite how many weeks, he had no idea. In the closed world of Kemble Place he had lost all sense of the passage of time.

He wondered what was happening now, what people were doing, what Bryony was doing. He felt oddly attached to the house in spite of everything, found himself hoping that the fire had destroyed no more than the top floor. He thought of the butterflies and moths pinned to the cork boards in their cabinets. They too must have secured a release of sorts.

Despite the cool of the evening air he felt hot and sweaty. His legs ached from the effort of wading through sand and shingle in high heels. He wiped his damp forehead on the sleeve of his costume, smearing it with make-up. After a while, his breathing became more even. The distant susurration of wave on shore had a calming, soothing effect. He felt sleep overcoming him until a giggle and a gasp from behind the huts told him that it was time to move on.

He clattered along the board walk, still clutching his hat, past houses leaking comfort and warm yellow light. A face at a window, a cat on a wall. From time to time, he turned to look behind, just to make sure. Still nothing, no one. He reached the cottages; the Mermaid was in sight. Outside Ocean View, a lamp post, one of the old-fashioned sort with a lantern at the top. More Narnia than Sanderling, he thought, as he was absorbed by its muted glow; no sign of Mr Tumnus or anyone else.

"Like the tights." He started at the sudden intrusion. It was one of the girls just leaving the cottage next door. "They match the feather. Fancy dress, is it?" They sniggered off into the semi-darkness without waiting for an answer. She had a point, though. How could he wander into town looking like this?

The donkey shop was where he thought it was. He had followed alleys and quiet back lanes in an effort to avoid quips and stares in the high street. The glazed door at the front rattled and shook as he pushed it; it was as unyielding as he had expected. Was there another way in? The donkey in the poster on the door, sporting straw hat and sun glasses, was giving nothing away.

He edged past wheelie bins to the peeling side gate, open a crack, too warped and swollen to be locked shut. It gave on to a small paved area at the back of the shop. As he crept forward, he collided with two plastic chairs, angled against a table to deflect the rain. He ducked behind the gate in case the noise had attracted unwelcome attention. But no one seemed to have heard it.

At the rear of the building, another door, lacking a handle or any other means of releasing it from the outside. But the shrouded window in the lean-to beyond gaped to reveal a murky slice of kitchen. The window rocked gently, held in place only by a loose brass stay. Colin lifted it with ease and pulled the window towards him. Placing one of the plastic chairs under the window, he threw his hat into the room and clambered on to the sill. The opening was not large but it was large enough for him to squeeze through, snagging his tights in the process.

He found himself on a work surface, laminated to give the crystalline effect of polished granite. He swung his legs round, narrowly avoiding the electric kettle but not the tin of biscuits that went crashing to the floor. Chocolate digestives rolled in several directions. He gathered as many as he could find and heaped them roughly in their misshapen tin. Of its lid, there was no sign.

He pulled the window to, just in case, and penetrated the body of the shop. It was hard to see but he could not afford to put a light on, could not take the risk of being caught now. He slid his hat on to the counter by the till, together with the good luck cards he had secreted about his person. He removed the rest of his Feste costume, and felt his way towards the racks of men's clothing. Through trial and error, he slowly pieced together jacket, shirt and trousers and found a pair of shoes that were not too uncomfortable, even without socks.

A loosely curtained doorway to the left of the counter led into a room for sorting, pricing and storing donated goods until they were transferred to the sales area. He fumbled past bales and bags and boxes until he reached another door, folded like a concertina, that revealed a small basin with bevelled mirror above. He reached for the light pull and slid the door to a close. With the aid of soap, water and a couple of hand towels he removed the worst of the blotched and smeary make-up that had made him look, he now realised, like a rasher of streaky bacon.

Back at the counter, he scooped his costume into a Fun Fashions carrier bag, picked up the hat and cards and prepared to leave. But what about money? The till was shut fast. The collection box, though, was reassuringly heavy. They must have forgotten to lock it away. He resolved to post some compensatory notes if and when he made it back home.

He reversed through the kitchen window, pushed it to and applied the knife he had found on the draining board. Slicing through the seal, he opened the box and filled his pockets with coins. He dumped box, bag and hat in a wheelie bin in the passage at the side and headed for the high street. The knife, he kept.

He wondered what time it was. The clock in the post office window said five past ten; the one in the bank claimed it was only five to. Either way, it was too late to catch a useful train from Sanderling, even assuming the bulges in his pockets would yield enough for the fare. But the first priority was to find a phone box, something he had never attempted since he acquired a mobile phone. There must be one somewhere, even now.

The station was a possibility but he did not want to traipse there on the off-chance. There might be a phone at the Mermaid but he had doubts about the reliability of the landlord and his wife, given their readiness to hand his overnight bag to Charles. He tried to remember whether he had seen one in the foyer of the leisure centre. He made his way towards the harbour. There, on the front: a carton of pale light balancing on the harbour's edge. He fished for coins and prepared to dial. The only number he could remember was the phone at twenty-six Mafeking Avenue, drummed into him in early childhood and never forgotten.

No reply. He let it ring and ring. There was no answer phone to intercept him and allow him to leave a message. Where were they? Could Clare and his father still be here, somewhere in the town? He had no way of knowing but it seemed unlikely. A couple of days had passed since Charles had overheard them in the donkey shop.

A sharp tap on the glass, an anxious face. He put down the phone and left, spluttering apologies.

The coins, he estimated, amounted to about twenty pounds. Surely not enough for a room for the night – even his tasteful Mermaid garret had cost more than that – or to get all the way home. Certainly not enough for both. What to do? He gazed forlornly at the fishermen's huts, dark and brooding across the water, and sighed.

"Long time no see." Something large and beige swayed towards him. He felt a hand on his shoulder.

Instinctively, he reached for the knife in the inside pocket of his jacket and turned towards his assailant. He reeled at the stench of gin and well-chewed cashews.

"Remember us? Ray, as in sunshine." A round puce face above a disordered paisley cravat. "And my good lady wife, Flo."

A small woman teetered behind and offered a quiet wave. Colin released the knife.

"Yes, of course. How are you?"

"You've heard the news," said Flo. "It's a tragedy."

He looked blank.

"The fire," said Ray. "At Kemble Place."

"It was like a beacon against the sky."

"We saw it from the Mermaid."

"Isn't that where Howard…?"

"It is…or was."

"Why, was the house badly damaged?"

"Mainly the top floor and the roof, according to Jim at the pub. His brother is a volunteer fireman."

"But Howard Desmond is missing. They say he went back into the building and up the stairs before anyone could stop him."

"Everyone else was outside on the lawn. Apparently, they had some play on; they were all in costume."

"Not that we were asked," said Flo.

"There wasn't an audience, dear."

"Perhaps it was just a dress rehearsal," said Colin.

"But who were the players and what will happen to the play? And what about Howard Desmond? After all those years in the business. It's a crime he never had a knighthood. I do hope Celerity Box will be made a Dame."

"It's time we were getting back. Good night, er…"

"Colin."

"That's right. Perhaps we might see you again at the Mermaid."

"I'm sure."

Ray led Flo gently by the elbow in the direction of the high street. Colin went back to the phone box, vacant again, steadied himself momentarily against the door, and began to press the buttons in front of him.

Seventeen

*I*t's Friday," said Mrs Nolan. "Have you forgotten? I'm here on a Friday."

"Pleasingly brown, then, like a beech leaf in winter." He slumped at the kitchen table and yawned. He had done little but sleep in the days since his return.

"Not that again. I'd have thought you might have got over it."

"I've always seen Fridays as turquoise," said Colin's mother, a tall, slim woman moving slowly, carefully into the kitchen. She was focussing on the vase of anemones she brought to the dresser. "Ever since I can remember."

"The saints preserve us," said Mrs Nolan. She snatched duster and polish and huffed into the sitting room.

They had been staying in Gadwall, his father and sister, a little up the coast from Sanderling. A small town, much favoured by artists, its choice as the Mallory's honeymoon destination thirty years or so before had attracted some derision at a time when more exotic locations were the order of the day. "It's so hole in corner. The Robinson's daughter had a fortnight in Mauritius." The drive down from Gadwall after they had the call from Oxbourne, the tearful reunion ("You've put on weight."), talking long into the night in their seafront hotel when all Colin wanted to do was go to bed.

The squaring of Mrs Nolan, it turned out, was nothing more than a message, purporting to be from Colin, that he was going to London to stay with Clare while he looked for work, accompanied by a generous advance for continuing to look after the house. His disappearance only became apparent when Clare rang one Friday morning some weeks later to remind him of their parents' imminent return and the need to ensure that the wine was replenished.

Eric and Janet Mallory had been for calling the police from the outset but Clare was convinced that Colin's absence was linked to his obsessive search for Bryony and his trip to Sanderling.

"That girl," said Mrs Mallory. "Nothing but trouble. I thought he'd forgotten her."

A visit to Bert had proved inconclusive. He no longer had the carrier bag, he said, exuding an aroma of sweat and toasted cheese on the threshold of Milton Lodge. But Clare had at least remembered the name of the shop. The woman in Fun Fashions recalled Colin and his dog-eared picture of Bryony with some amusement and was more forthcoming about offloading most of their bags on the donkey place. Clare and her father thus avoided a circuit as tortuous as Colin's own but the outcome was no more satisfactory. They took their argument about what to do to the Samphire Café, wedged in a corner with lobster chowder and a hunk of home-made bread.

It was clear that Colin had been here looking for Bryony. That much they agreed. Whether he had found her and where he was now was wholly obscure. Neither fancied wandering the streets with Colin's photograph, asking random passers-by if they had seen him. His track record in keeping in touch was scarcely exemplary so silence did not necessarily mean anything untoward and he could be considered old enough to look after himself. On the other hand, simply vanishing was not typical. Had he fallen under Bryony's spell or had her captors taken him too?

In the circumstances, there was, they felt, some merit in discretion. They settled on approaching a firm of private investigators, one practised in tracing missing persons, and resolved to seek out potential candidates once they were back in Oxbourne.

The *Sanderling Recorder* could now be viewed on-line. It was published every Thursday and Colin monitored it for reports of the fire at Kemble Place. Its cause was under investigation but foul play was not suspected. The damage, it seemed, was as limited as Ray had said, spectacular though the conflagration had been at the time. An inquest was to be held into the death of the well-known actor Howard Desmond, whose body had been found among the remains of the top-floor landing, lying underneath a charred beam presumed to have fallen from the roof.

His widow and long-time acting partner, Celerity Box, confirmed that all other occupants of the house were accounted for and that no one was missing. She told the *Recorder* that, in memory of Mr Desmond, a small company of actors would be performing Shakespeare's *Twelfth Night* at the Church Hall in Victoria Road. Dates would be announced once casting was completed.

Colin slid a twenty-pound note from his wallet and then a ten for good measure. He slipped both into a manila envelope, already stamped and bearing the address of a charity shop that nestled in a passageway close to Sanderling High Street. He sealed the envelope and told his mother that he was going to the post box on the corner of Mafeking Avenue and Jubilee Drive.

Eighteen

*I*t was September. A promising blue sky had given way to dull grey cloud, flecked with rain. Colin burst breathless out of the station lift, through the turnstiles and into the street ahead. Even he could not face the prospect of climbing a hundred and ninety-three steps.

He hesitated, looked about him, and headed towards the piazza. He was early, having misjudged the time it would take to get here from Clare's north London flat. He had come up from Oxbourne the day before and spent the night, just to make sure. An interview with a language school, he had said. True enough, but not until late that afternoon.

He slid over wet cobbles, dodging groups of tourists, shifting and shapeless, some sporting policemen's helmets, others lurid in jester's cap and bells. He took shelter in a broad arcade, rapidly enveloped by scents of chocolate, lavender and rose seeping from nearby shops. From somewhere behind him, the sounds of a string quartet, a little night music beyond the market stalls.

Idle googling had brought him here. The obituaries themselves had been and gone some months before, polite rather than reverential, brief surveys of a long career, uniformly light about the final years, uniformly illustrated with grainy pictures of a much younger man wearing panama and pencil moustache as Anton in *The Olive Grove*, an older one wild and haggard as Lear in a stormy scene set upon a heath. A new site, developed and maintained by loyal fans Ray and Flo, announced that Howard Desmond's memorial service would be taking place today at noon.

Colin knew he bore some responsibility for the fact that it was taking place at all. He had started the fire that had led to the actor's death. But any guilt he had felt when reading the account in the *Sanderling Recorder* was tempered by the simple point that Howard Desmond had had no compunction in imprisoning him at Kemble Place and threatening him with dire consequences if he did not cooperate. Desmond had brought it upon himself. At the very least, he thought, if Bryony and the others shared responsibility for his capture and confinement they surely shared responsibility for Desmond's death too. The good luck cards, a trifle battered and rubbed, remained at the back of his sock drawer.

He lurked and paced and lurked again. A juggler, dwarfed by the sombre portico of the church opposite, attracted a small but growing crowd, their enthusiasm undiminished by the stiffening drizzle, oblivious of the figures passing slowly, quietly through the rusticated gateway at the side. Some in respectful black, others more colourfully dressed in celebration of a lifetime in the theatre, most half-hidden by umbrellas of unusual variety. One, he thought, in denim suit and apricot shirt could have been Ken Westow but it was hard to tell.

He looked at the large gold hands of the clock centred in the massive pediment. It was nearly time. He switched off the mobile phone bulging in his pocket, the same phone returned with his watch and credit cards a few weeks ago, carefully wrapped inside a jiffy bag and slipped through the letter box at number twenty-six. No name, no note, nothing to identify the sender. It was there on the mat when he came back from a walk through the woods, curious to see what was happening at Milton Lodge, a prospect of scaffolding and skips as the place was gradually made habitable for the new owners. Of matters Bertish there was no sign, save the dog-eared catalogue of 'Naughty But Nice' lying twisted and swollen in a puddle by the laurel hedge.

Glancing to left and right, he skirted the crowd and slithered through the gate, past dripping trees and damp benches inscribed with names he did not know. The whistles and whoops and claps from the square receded, replaced by a medley of tunes from *Salad Days* sounding from the body of the church. As he mounted the steps and approached a pair of glass doors, the music stopped, supplanted by the mournful toll of a single bell. He slipped inside; another set of glass doors confronted him. If there had been a receiving line, it had now dispersed, places taken among the rows of heads and hats in pews.

He saw the rector rise to welcome the assembled company. The church looked packed but there was no one he could identify at this distance. Surely she would be here, sitting at the front with Celerity Box and other former inmates of Kemble Place?

A grey-haired woman, stooping to stroke a tabby cat, straightened to offer him the last remaining service sheet.

"You're welcome to go in."

His nerve failed him. He retreated to the gardens in front of the church and pulled the service sheet from his pocket. It was bound in a stiff cream cover, deckle-edged, decorated with the masks of Tragedy and Comedy and a few words printed in maroon, or possibly burgundy. 'Howard George Merryweather Desmond,' he read. '*Every inch a king.*'

He made his way to a covered passage off to the side of the churchyard, past a scattering of fans in anoraks nursing playbills and autograph books beneath protective polythene. He glanced, with little interest, at notices and flyers fixed loosely to the wall. He wondered how long the service would take, how long he had before... . A car door slammed in the street beyond, heels echoed sharply on the worn stone floor and suddenly stopped.

" '*What country, friends, is this?*' " The voice was warm and familiar.

He turned and smiled. " '*This is Illyria, Lady.*' "

Epilogue

Colin kept walking, a meandering circuit through streets and squares, elegant and restrained. The day was becoming brighter, more clearly defined. The low grumble of Parisian traffic was now a steady roar. How long had he been? Time enough before they had to be at the diminutive Théâtre Marivaux, a crumbling space, all gilt and plum velours, a former warehouse wedged in an alley off the Rue Marianne, not far from the Gare du Nord. Rehearsals were now underway for Ken Westow's English-language production of *Love's Labours Lost*. It was to take the place of his current success with *Much Ado About Nothing*, in which Bryony reprised the role of Hero to much acclaim. Colin, on trial as Dogberry ('*O that I had been writ down an ass!*'), was promoted in the new production to play the King of Navarre, opposite Bryony as the Princess of France.

The Kemble Players, he had been told, were disbanded after the final performance of *Twelfth Night*, Celerity

Box having decided to reassign roles among the remaining members of the cast. She dispensed with Fabian and gave the part of Feste to Cornelia Thrupp, with mixed results. Kemble Place had reverted to its former name and was to become The Red House Hotel and Conference Centre once works of construction and reconstruction were complete.

Against expectations, Celerity Box had repaid Bryony and Charity much of the money they had lent to Howard Desmond; she was now settled in a large flat overlooking Battersea Park, not far from the smaller flat from which Cornelia and Brenda ran Periwinkle Domestic Cleaning Services. Charity had pooled resources with her brother Bert and bought a bungalow in the same Devon village as their elder siblings, Faith and Hope.

The family were bewildered that Colin could take up once again with someone who had tricked him and apparently shown little remorse and throw away any prospect of a proper job for one he had previously condemned as ephemeral and insubstantial. Had he learned nothing from his reckless behaviour? His explanation that it would be different this time did not convince them. But the fact was that, for all the rage and frustration at his confinement, and fears for his safety after James Dudley's death came to light, he had rather enjoyed being a member of a group, each with a clearly defined role, but working together to make the play. Whether those fears were really justified, or just part of Howard Desmond's plan to focus his mind and encourage cooperation, he never knew and had not asked, preferring to look forward rather than back and make the best of things as they were or seemed to be.

When Ken made the offer in the pub after the memorial service, he jumped at the chance to join Bryony and the Enigma troupe in Paris for a couple of months. If the money was derisory and the future obscure, he still had an inheritance to fall back on. As did Bryony. And now there was a real audience to support, encourage, cajole, deride, as the mood took them. The only certainty was the unpredictability of their reaction: ecstatic one night, coolly polite the next, for no reason that those on stage could make out. Disconcerting, perhaps, but better by far than the pre-programmed response of the dummies of Kemble Place.

The sun emerged as he neared the Rue des Bouffons. The daily queue from the *boulangerie artisanale* curled round the corner to the neighbouring street; he thought of coffee, croissants and freshly baked bread. A sudden gust brought dry leaves twirling, swirling to the entrance of the hotel; they were a pleasing orange-brown in the warm morning light. A Friday colour, he thought, as he picked up a leaf and went inside.